Leaves

FROM THE VALLEY OAK

VISALIA-EXETER WRITERS' 2011 ANTHOLOGY

A collection of short stories, poems, creative
non-fiction, memoir and inspirational writings
by
Visalia-Exeter Writers.

Produced by
Visalia-Exeter Writers
Exeter, California, USA

Compiled and edited by
Mary Benton and Gloria Getman

Cover Art
Graphics by Sylvia Ross
Photography by Gloria Getman

Printed in the USA
Copies available through Amazon.com
or by contacting individual authors

ISBN-13:978-0-9854747-3-7

Visalia and Exeter Writers
2011

Dedication

Mary Martin Benton

1938 – 2015

Mary Benton was a valued member of the Visalia-Exeter Writer's Critique Group from its inception. A talented writer and tough critic, her comments and corrections kept us on the path to publication. Her many stories and books entertained us, made us laugh, and inspired us to become better writers. As co-editor for this anthology, her encouragement and enthusiasm were essential to bring this book to completion.

ACKNOWLEDGMENTS

Special thanks to Arthur Neeson for his tireless pursuit to secure satisfactory meeting places for our writers' groups. His unfailing posts to remind us of the times and location, and his steady encouragement are greatly appreciated.

Gloria Getman for her dedication to this project, and the endless hours she spent on compiling the stories, poems, memoirs, and inspirational writings that has resulted in our first anthology.

Sylvia Ross for the layout and cover design, and the distinctive logo that simply "says it all." Thanks, Sylvia, for this valuable gift.

To each of the authors who contributed their time, efforts and their very best works to make this book a success. Thank you.

TABLE OF CONTENTS

MY GRANDMA WAS A HUCKABY

By
Winnie Enloe Furrer

True Stories of California History from
William Huckaby's Pioneering Family

DEDICATION

This section is dedicated to all Huckaby and Pollard relatives who reaffirmed our family stories and helped with the alignment of birth, marriage and death dates.

A special thanks to my aunt, Betty Jean Pollard Neely, who acted as an editor by answering my calls for assistance day or night.

The Huckaby family
Mattie, William, Henry, Margie, Martha, Wesley
and Etta

PROLOGUE

William Huckaby was born on February 5, 1858, to David Huckaby and Margie Akers Huckaby in Centerville, California. He and a brother moved to Southern California during their teenage years. He met and married young Martha Ann Casteel on June 27, 1880, in Riverside.

Twenty-two-year-old William was a small wiry young man with black curly hair. Although rather quiet with an unusually soft voice, he acted with a will of steel. He allowed only black and white and displayed little tenderness.

He was raised in a farming community which at that time provided little formal schooling. Math came easily to him and seemed to give him an eye for aligning furrows and orchards. Many farmers sought him to layout and plant their orchards and vineyards. William was asked to oversee the planting of palm trees which still stand on Palm Avenue in Riverside.

Their income was not steady and the family moved often since these jobs were not permanent. He soon realized his family could make a fairly good living by clearing land for cultivation if they lived on the acreage during the process. So began their nomadic life as their family grew to seven members.

SIN WITHIN THE HEART

The desert sun washed its own reflection in the canal's water as the Huckaby's wagon passed over the bridge that evening onto the land they would call home for some months. Tall arrow-weed lined the trail onto the new land hiding the warm muddy water and mosquitoes humming for blood.

Ol' Dan, a horse whose age was depicted by his name, would help as the notion nudged him. After a lot of wasted time getting him over the bridge, William felt sure Ol' Dan was really a mule in disguise.

"Come on, Henry," William called to his son. "Unharness the horse and stake the animals. Girls, start cutting down the arrow-weed to clear out a living area. Don't worry about snakes or lizards, Etta. All of our commotion will make 'um run."

Arrow-weed, a tall variety of arrow-wood, is found in Mexico and the southwestern part of the United States. Indians used these strong slender stalks to make arrows and to build their homes.
These plants were an important part of building their new living quarters so William quickly asked his wife, Martha, to oversee the stacking of brush. He chose a spot to set up camp which was close enough to the canal to put water within fetching distance and yet far enough away to discourage mosquitoes.

As each member of the family finished their assigned tasks, they helped the girls. The clearing was made large enough for bedrolls and a fire before dark. Martha directed the unloading of the wagon. Everyone hoped their activities would keep snakes away for the night. But Martha and her second daughter, Etta, hoped for lizards to be frightened by their activities. Their uncontrollable fear kept them awake and searching for small yellow eyes throughout the moonless night. New noises of crickets, coyotes, and only God knew what else, created a restless first night in their new home. Dawn lessened their fear and brought the entire family into action.

Martha roused reluctant youngsters, readied cooking gear over mesquite wood and soon had the aroma of fried onions with yesterday's boiled potatoes filling the camp. Eggs scrambled, biscuits lifted from the ashes, God thanked, and the morning meal was wolfed down. On this day they would build their new tent-home. They would start their field work on the very next day.

The stacked arrow-weed from the night before had now grown to a very large pile of neatly laid brush. The girls continued to enlarge the living area as William and Henry built the tree limb framework. It surrounded an area of approximately twelve by twenty-four feet. The roof was completed by tying the arrow-weed in small bundles to the top of the cross-beams, or uprights.

William and his son would determine the thickness that would keep out the sun and rain. All sides were left open to catch any breeze. An eight-by-eight foot tent was erected under one corner of the covered framework. It was used for dressing, bathing and sleeping on cooler nights.

Martha and the girls created a cooking area in the open portion of the covered space. The cooking fire itself was kept outside of the roof. Bedrolls, iron pots and skillets, garlic, children and God, established their new home.

Work day started long before sunup. Martha baked biscuits, cooked mush and fried eggs by lantern before dawn so that everyone could be in the fields by daybreak. They all wanted to beat the heat. "Everyone up!" she called as she started the open fire. Although Martha had a soft voice, no one questioned her authority.

Assigned chores kept each member working toward the collective goal. Etta, their second daughter, was told to fix the lunches and to put them in the cooler. The cooler was a wire box covered by wet canvas and hung from the tent house framework to keep food eatable until mid-day.

Marjorie, who was the oldest child, was to assist Martha with breakfast, put away the bedrolls and rake the floor. When the dust layer wore away, Marjorie could then sweep the hard earth clean.

To Mattie, the youngest child, she said, "You clean up the dishes and cooking gear and feed the chickens." Mattie was glad she got to feed the chickens because she hated the cow. She hated its tail, constant chewing, and the flies.

The tent-house was straightened and everyone took turns feeding the large animals as Henry helped his father prepare for the day's work.

Here in the late 1890's protection was a necessary part of clothing. Cuts from cruel thorny tumble weeds on the desert floor could lead to infection. Everyone wore gloves and wide brimmed hats. Henry and his father wore collarless shirts with rolled up sleeves over their perpetual long-johns. Each worker carried a large bandanna to wear around the lower part of their face against the dust. Since a lady's skin must be white, Martha and the girls wore men's shirts over their ankle-length dresses. Only field workers' arms and faces were tanned by the harsh desert sun. No lady wanted to be identified as a field hand.

Before sunup Ol' Dan pulled yesterday's cuttings into a cleared area where they would be burned. Etta and Mattie watched the fire and used the longest sticks they could find to pull any airborne fireballs back into their crematory. Both girls hoped the fire would be out before full sun gave birth to the heat. The desert heat magnified the pungent smells of sage, mesquite, insects, rabbits, snakes and anything else rotting in the old seabed's penetrating dust.

"Mattie, leave that snake alone." Etta feared snakes and lizards as uncontrollably as her mother, but she could not stand to see anything tortured.

"I want to watch it burn. I'm trying to flip it into the fire."

"Don't Mattie! Please don't! Look at the poor thing."

"Etta, it's on fire. We'll have to burn it now. You don't want to see it suffer, do you?"

It stood on its tail, and its tongue darted its message for mercy and waved in a fiery pattern as it struggled for oxygen, only to be tossed in the fire once more by Mattie's long stick. Suddenly Etta's breakfast covered her dress and the ground in front of her. The snake no longer struggled.

Martha bent over her hoe, tearing out weeds long lodged in the hard earth. She was a short, stout woman in her thirties. Their hard life was etched in her lined face and fading hair. The small dark eyes sparkled with a direct, friendly gaze. They were framed in a pleasing square face.

She constantly watched for lizards. Although it was common knowledge they were friendly once they got on someone, Martha's fear consumed her. She could not tolerate the thought of these common desert inhabitants crawling on her or one of her children.

Mattie and Henry chased all lizards, stomping on their long spiny tails and laughing as the frightened lizards ran off leaving their tails wiggling under the children's feet. They were careful to practice the sport only when their mother or Etta were elsewhere.

Evening brought a slight breeze. Martha straightened her aching back. She caught the fragile touch of the desert's cooled breath and found that it was both relaxing and invigorating. *I'll hoe a few more large bushes and then start back to begin supper.*

She bent again, looked down toward the brush and saw the yellow, saucy-eyed, cocked head of a LIZARD! Its tongue darted out toward her and it seemed to smile at her from the brim of her own hat. *My Lord! The creature is actually on me. The filthy little picture of hell is right in my face. Help me! Yellow eyes and darting tongues are exploding into millions of little spiny-tailed devils. They are completely covering me!*

In one continuous motion the round, buxom woman screamed, jumped, turned and flung the poisonous hat as though it would swallow her. Screams purged her throat with every breath as her short legs raced for the tent. With each scream she tore her clothing and stripped each piece from her body. She ripped free of the button-less shirt. She tripped on her dress as it slipped down her hips. The infected bodice was also flung to the ground. She was free of clothes and still she could feel claws and smell the arid

9

creature's desert odor. Her large pale breasts flopped wildly with each step. Her terrorized flight seemed to intensify her own fear. She was left with only large work shoes. Long, fading hair trailed the pale, vibrating buttocks of nude Martha Casteel Huckaby as she plunged the remaining distance to the tent. Her frightened family raced after her but didn't catch her before she disappeared into their tent.

As William tried to question Martha, her convulsive sobbing only confused him more. "Why did you expose yourself? You know that you've sinned." He could not understand why her sacrilegious act seemed to mean nothing to her. Henry and Mattie thought the whole thing funny but degrading. Marjorie was mortified. Only Etta understood her mother's actions.

Martha was never able to make William understand and forgive her for exposing her nude body to her children and the world. She remained a sinner, not only in her own heart, but in her husband's heart as well.

THE FINALE

About 1890 an absentee farmer hired William to ready the ground and plant some additional acreage to enlarge his orange orchard and grape vineyard.

When the farmer returned and made his final inspection, he was impressed with William's ability to align both the young orange trees and the grape cuttings. He hired the young wiry Mormon to oversee these young plants to maturity. The job came complete with a house. This was his first job that gave his family a steady income and a home. His family gratefully moved into their one-bedroom, unpainted house in Moreno Valley, California.

Martha quietly reminded William that they needed their own cow. William bought a cow, Bess, from their closest neighbor. He also traded their unneeded ground-clearing gear for a young hog heavy with piglets. The seller threw in a few baby chickens, three hens and a huge rooster.

That rooster became William's pride and joy. It was a Rhode Island Red. From the first day on the farm he was simply called Rooster. He immediately took control of the chicken yard and soon ruled the pig pen and then began pestering the cow.

When he discovered the children were afraid of him, he began silently launching attacks on any one of the children crossing his yard. With head lowered, feathers fluffed, wings slightly spread and, it seemed, spurs sharpened, he would charge directly toward his prey with amazing speed. After the girls ran and reacted with screams, and Henry yelled cuss words as he threw anything handy, Rooster would strut and crow with an arrogant lilt in his voice.

"Has anyone seen Rooster?" William asked the family one Monday just before breakfast. All five children and Martha indicated they had not seen him, and in fact, Martha was rather pleased that the ornery, prideful thing was no longer in the yard. Now maybe she could let Wesley, their youngest, outside to play without watching him every second.

"Well, I'm afraid he's wandered off. I want everyone to keep an eye out for him. I'll ask the neighbors to watch for him too. Who's going to say grace?"

Unexpectedly Henry volunteered. The girls looked at him knowing that whatever had happened to Rooster, Henry was behind it. No one said an accusing word. Etta and Mattie elbowed one another, but Marjorie cautioned the girls with a scowl.

The week went by with a new air of carefree activity. The girls actually forgot to look for old Rooster as they did chores and walked to and from school. Martha could hang clothes and take her youngest outside with no fear of the dreaded bird and his razor-sharp spurs. "I hope he has received his just reward. Nothing should be that spiteful and prideful and not receive its due." Martha was heard to say.

One week to the day after Rooster disappeared, William headed out to the family two-holer right after dinner. He noticed Henry had done a nice job of clearing weeds around the outhouse. Maybe he should tell Henry how nice it looked. He hadn't even asked Henry to do the work.

Seconds after he entered the outhouse, he burst out again yelling at the top of his voice, "Henry! Where is that boy? Henry! Girls! Where is your brother? Martha, where is your son?"

"We'll find him, Papa," Etta called. She grabbed Mattie's hand and headed for the old orchard. Her one long, dark-brown braid bounced from side to side. "Come on, Mattie. We've got to find Henry first. I know he won't come in by himself."

William was a member in good standing of the Reorganized Church of Jesus Christ of Latter Day Saints. None of the children had ever heard him raise his voice in anger. Even Martha was surprised by his outburst.

"What is it, William?" she called as she ran toward him, wiping her hands on her flour-sack apron. Martha looked around for Henry and the girls. "Where are the children? What's happened?"

"When I find that son of yours, there will be tarnation to pay. He can't treat another living creature like that." As he stopped to breathe, Marjorie and Martha looked up at his red face. His mustache twitched, and his small round eyes appeared to bug out of his face. "Henry will get Rooster out of that two-holer and he will clean that bird up and Henry will repent!"

"Now William, don't get so upset," Martha cautioned as she touched his shoulder.

"I'm already upset, woman. Don't tell me not to get upset. Where is Henry? I know he did it. I know he put Rooster down the outhouse. That rooster is still alive down there floundering around. I know it. I hung the lantern down there and I saw him."

Marjorie and Martha held their faces in their aprons. It would not due to have Papa see them smile, or worse yet, laugh.

Etta found Henry sitting under an orange tree in the old orchard. She and Mattie convinced Henry that he'd better come before Papa got any madder.

Henry had heard him and couldn't believe his father's anger. "All over a mean old rooster. I thought he'd be dead by now. Only something from the devil could live down there in that crap. He's evil. He should have died."

Henry walked slowly towards his father as William stood stock-still with his fists clinched at his side. When Henry stood directly in front of his father, he said, "Yes. I thought I killed your old Rooster. He spurred me, so I grabbed him by the neck and threw him down the outhouse. He's mean. He could have hurt one of the girls, or the baby."

"So you judged him and passed sentence on him? You, a ten year old boy, are so wise that God has granted you this gift of judgment?"

"I thought he deserved it."

"Well, let me tell you what God gave me. God gave me children to raise, and he granted me judgment to accomplish that important job. And with that judgment, I tell you it is wrong to treat any living thing like you treated that bird. I judge you guilty of abusing Rooster, and you will rescue him. You will climb down there and pull him out of that mire. You will wash him clean and set him free on firm ground in the fresh air again. Do you hear me, Henry?"

"Yes sir!"

"Here's the lantern. Watch out for spiders." William turned and with both arms gathered the rest of his family and turned them toward the house. Henry was left alone by the outhouse to carry out his penance.

He knew there was no way other than sudden death to get out of this dreadful chore. *How can I get this done the fastest, easiest way and still have it hurt the least? I'll try a rope. … Oh, shit! The damn rope slid off.*

At last he took off all his home-made clothes, except his long underwear. It was Monday and all his clothes were clean. He did not want to get anything from that shit-pit on them. He sat the clothes carefully on a nearby tree stump and raised the bench seat. He slid down into the depth of stench which filled that hell hole. He hoped that he could hold his breath long enough to pick up that damnable bird.

One good grab and he had the skinny, slimy devil in his hand. He threw the bird in a short arc, and it sailed out the hole on the first try. As Henry was pulling himself up, the bird staggered out of the outhouse and into clean, sweet air once again. Henry watched it reel as it tried to flap its dung-covered wings and pollute everything around him. Rooster finally stretched his neck to its limit and let out a raspy crow which brought the entire family back into the yard. As his crow subsided, the rooster seemed to swoon and fall to the ground. The bird quivered as his claws tried to grasp for a firm grip in the rich earth. Then he was still.

"God be praised," Martha said quietly.

BIG GIRLS DON'T CRY

The year of 1892 brought the Huckaby children their very best Christmas. All three girls received homemade nightgowns which Martha made from brightly-colored flour sacks. She made Papa and Henry new house shoes from sugar sacks. Henry also got his own shovel. Baby Wesley received a few toys bought in town, and also a new nightshirt made of the same material as the girls' dresses. Eight-year-old Etta and six-year-old Mattie received brand-new doll buggies. Margie, at twelve, told the youngest girls she was much too adult to play with dolls. She received a beautiful new hair brush.

The younger ones didn't care. The small replicas of grown-up buggies were the most marvelous things the girls had ever owned. They were made of bright yellow wicker and even had rubber tires. Each had a hood that turned to the front or back to shade their baby dolls. Mama made a mattress for each buggy from old towels. They took turns pushing baby Wesley in the buggies around the yard after chores. Wesley loved it. He was perfectly content to let his big sisters take turns at playing mama.

By the end of June, 1893, the young vines were producing a few grapes. William's family was happy, and he was confident that they would have a good first crop within a couple of years.

Martha found him in the yard and interrupted his thoughts by asking him if he had seen Wesley. "The Children have called and looked everywhere."

William, who had just left the orange grove, said, "I'll check the grapes. He's so short, maybe they couldn't see him. Wesley knows he shouldn't be there so he probably isn't answering."

Every member of the household had been looking for some time when William came carrying him home. He had found Wesley eating his fill of unripe wine grapes.

Etta retold the story many times of how his white middy blouse, short blue trousers, bare feet and smiling face were covered with the bright purple juice and how his big brown eyes shown from successfully hiding from his family.

By evening diarrhea began. Diarrhea plagued little Wesley with painful cramps for days. There were few doctors in Moreno Valley at that time and none could be reached to help Wesley. As days dragged on, William ground carob beans for Martha to make a medicinal drink for the child. The carob bean has been known as a binding substance for the bowels, however, it did not help. As he doubled up with cramps, his stool became pure blood.

Wesley died July 9, 1893. His death certificate declares "Bloody Flux" as the cause of death. He was four years, four months and two days old.

Each member of the family was devastated and felt guilty for not finding him sooner, especially his big brother and sister, Henry and Margie. They, as teen-agers, had already learned to hide grief and guard against tears. Etta and Mattie could not stop theirs. Both buggies were empty and the small family dog would not play baby. Wesley could not be replaced. They found it impossible to find closure on their little brother's death.

After a few months, William could no longer be content surrounded by familiar reminders of his son's death. Martha watched William and feared he was thinking of moving again. She watched him walk with pride among the small trees in the new orchard. She knew he wanted to fulfill his commitment to the new plants, but struggled with his loss of young Wesley. Oh, how she prayed she was wrong.

She started evaluating the few things they had accumulated since they settled in a real house. She fondled a chair, caressed the iron-black cook stove that belonged to the house. She loved that stove. There was an understanding between them on how to set the right temperature on whatever Martha wanted to cook.

One afternoon as the children arrived home from school, they overheard Papa talking to Mama as she hung clothes. "Martha, it's time to move on. I can't seem to fight off my memories of the little one here. Every one of us should have known where the baby was playing. I was much too harsh with him." He paused and looked east beyond the grape vines. "We'll go to Yuma again. I can work with my father." He turned and walked into the orchard. They knew that what their father had just said would be the last they would ever hear of their shame or guilt. Each of them knew that they would silently carry their guilt for the rest of their life like a sack of soured grits tied tightly on their backs.

Moving meant each Huckaby must take only the few necessities that fit in or on the wagon. Martha would leave furniture and any accumulation of sewing material and other things not needed to survive or to earn money. All toys would be given away or left behind for the next occupant. The trip would be hard on the cow, but Martha knew Bess would move with them. Martha found a few of Wesley's new toys and hid them in with her long, black stockings.

Etta told Mattie she felt they were deserting Wesley. This house, his grave and the yard where they played belonged to the baby. They made a pact to do everything they could to take the buggies which reminded them so much of their baby brother.

The girls sat on the steps with arms folded over their calico-covered knees. Their braided heads were buried in their arms.

"Don't cry. You're big girls and big girls don't cry," cautioned their mother in her low voice. "Your father knows best. There is no place in the wagon to put your buggies. Be good now."

"Mama, we can push them," Etta pleaded through tears.

"Yes! Oh, Mama, please say we can," whined Mattie.

"All the way to Yuma? You girls must not remember what the desert is like. You both know your job is to walk ahead of the wagon to toss any snakes out of the tracks to protect the horses, don't you?"

"Yes, but we can push the buggies up front and look for snakes at the same time. We promise to keep our eyes on the tracks, and we won't miss any snakes. And we'll hold the buggies over the side of the wagon when it's our turn to ride. Talk to Papa. Please Mama," cried Etta. She could not explain the fullness in her chest that felt like Mama's big ball of string. But she knew it was all rolled up with her need to hold on to this last bit of Wesley.

"You two cannot push those buggies through the sand all the way to Yuma! The older two have their chores, so they cannot help you."

There was a pause as Martha turned and looked sternly at the two stubborn girls. "All right. I'll ask your father just to keep you two quiet. But don't count your chickens too soon." Tears dried and smiles appeared instantly as the girls jumped up and ran to tell Henry and Margie the news.

They knew their papa would at least let them try. They were right. He could no longer resist their courage.

Early the next morning they followed the worn path to Beaumont where they would start following the Southern Pacific Railroad. The Southern Pacific had completed its extension to Yuma in 1877. This extension would allow them to rest during the heat of the day under shady railroad trestles, and travel during the evening and even some nights. They had a little over 200 miles to travel.

When they left Palm Springs the girls walked their two miles before the sun cast a full shadow. They dragged the buggies for the last mile. William sighed as he watched his daughters' determined grasp on their last tie with Wesley. They pushed, pulled and dragged the buggies, first with one arm and then the other.

As Etta and Mattie took turns to rest, they each clung to the handle of their buggy as it hung over the side of the dust-covered wagon. Their long, black stockings and high-topped button shoes were now silt-brown. They smiled to themselves because they knew Wesley was going with them.

The family rested in Coachella and took on water as the children played with the many shells found around the hot artisan wells.

The trail along the railroad was hot and windy in October during the day, and very cool during the night. Lanterns were carried far into the night. Etta, being the older of the two, carried the lantern most of the night. Her other hand still clutched the buggy. She was not able to carry the long stick used to flick snakes from the wagon tracks and away from the horse's legs.

The loss of a horse in this country could possibly mean the loss of an entire family, so Mattie had to roust any sleeping rattlers.

Their upper lips were a dirty brown from breathing in the dust made by horse's hooves and their own feet. The smell of horse dung, sweat and railroad ties filled their lungs. Tired feet never left the dust.

After leaving Mecca, the wagon soon came into Dry Lake Basin. Sometimes Papa called it Lake Cahuilla and showed them the old water lines on the western mountains of when water had once filled the basin. He said that the basin had been dry for centuries. What looked like snow as far as a man could see was actually salt. It was this salt which brought the railroad to the new Liverpool Salt Company Mine at the north end of Salt or Dry Lake Basin.

Salton was the name of the station where the railroad cars were loaded with salt and sent all over the world. Salton boasted another artesian well that was free of salt. The water was cool and sweet. They filled every vessel that could hold water.

It was time to travel totally by night. The tracks they were following would take them along the east edge of Salton Sink. The railroad maintained watering stops at places such as Volcano, Old Beach, Flowing Wells, Mamouth, Mesquite, Glamis, Cactus, Ogilby and Pilot Knob. The water in these cement cisterns had been hauled from Coachella Valley and would provide all the water needed during the entire trip. The temperature could reach 120 degrees, but that was not likely at this time of year. The children had been over this trail before when William had followed his father to Yuma for work.

Martha and William prepared them for the next night's camp. "Remember the last time we traveled to Yuma?" William asked. "Do you recall that after the Salt Basin we came to the large mud volcanoes and paint pots?"

The children had been nodding sleepily, but their eyes suddenly sprang wide at the mention of volcanoes. Each child had memories of the frightening hot, steaming mud and the horrible smell that became obvious long before they reached shaky ground. "Well, we will be camping there again. I want you to remember the dangers." He shook a stick at them to emphasize his seriousness.

"Now remember children," Martha said, smoothing her apron, "stay close and step lightly. In the morning before we turn in, we'll explore a little so you can see all the colors before we move on. We don't want you going off on your own, do we Papa? Do you hear me, Henry?"

Once they became used to the strong sulfur smell, they had a marvelous adventure. For as far as they could see there was steam bubbling from the ground. In one section there were colors that changed like chameleons before their eyes. The blues and reds were bright and there were light yellowish-green bubbles with grey blending in. Someone long before had laid wide boards to walk over unstable ground. Henry was the first brave one to venture out. Soon, even Margie was running on the boards to find new colors. That evening it was time to move on.

As they followed the tracks, the buggies were no longer yellow. The wheels wobbled and the wicker broke in several places. The girls fought their battle without help. The first night after leaving the volcanoes, during their rest period, Etta fell asleep and dropped her buggy. Mattie jumped down to rescue the treasure. They were tired victors.

Then they came to the large silky hills where the sand became finer and deeper. Wagon ruts blew away with the wind. Everything became the color of the ageless sea-bottom surrounding them. The desert was a hard taskmaster.

Mattie's buggy became stuck in the sand. The wheels, which were no longer round, were completely buried. The tired fighter was still trying to free it as the wagon rolled by. Her father called for her to hurry ahead to her sister. "Mattie, you could get lost in this. Hurry now!"

Henry turned his horse around and shouted for Mattie to get up front. He kept her in sight as he continued to ride behind the wagon. Etta heard her father's call and dashed to her sister's side, also ignoring her brother's warning. She wasn't afraid. She could see the wagon.

By this time the buggy was hopelessly stuck and the wagon was still moving ahead without them. Etta knew they must now leave Wesley. He would understand. She didn't want her buggy if

Mattie was to lose hers. She placed her buggy right next to Mattie's, turned and took her sobbing sister in her arms and said, "Don't cry, Mattie. See, I put them together so they won't ever be lonely. Big girls don't cry." She placed her hands on Mattie's shoulders, looked deeply into her eyes and vowed, "When we grow up, I'll buy you a beautiful carriage and let you keep it always. Come on, we must catch the wagon." Etta grasped Mattie's little hand in hers as they hurried into their place in front of the horse.

No one looked back.

LITTLE IRON ASS

When the Huckaby family returned to California, jobs were still hard to find. William decided again to join the wagon people who followed the farm crops throughout California's valleys. His children, now in their teens, were all good workers. Etta had become known as a skilled worker at sulfuring grapes. The family was well received by growers as they arrived with other wagon people ready to go to work.

The moon was still visible in the early pre-dawn. Men in the camp made sure the equipment was ready for the day's disking in the orange grove. Boys fed the stock before harnessing them for the workday and women were busy preparing breakfast. Newly sharpened disks blades glistened with moisture, waiting silently to turn the rich soil of the Coachella desert floor.

William's cry of pain split the stillness, and Martha immediately burst from their nearby tent. She found one of the gleaming disks a blood-red under her husband as he tried to lift his body from the row of disc harrows. His right buttock seemed cut to the bone.

As his wife and son, Henry, tried to lift him, he ordered Henry to, "Get Doc Pollard now!"

Doc was already headed toward the injured man. The tall, burly doctor was three steps ahead of Henry on the way back to the harrow. He easily lifted the small, injured man and carried him to a hastily made pallet. He laid William on his left side. Doc's strong hands ripped the torn trousers to reveal the entire wound. Sunlight had brightened the camp, allowing Doc to better inspect William's injured buttock. The cut resembled a deep slice in a bleeding rump roast. No major arteries or veins appeared severed.

Pollard shouted commands in a military style which left no questions. "Enola! Get our Indian Tea and boil lots of water. Mrs. Huckaby, get me the largest needle you can find and thread, linen thread if you have it. If you don't, bring me anything you have that's white – and clean. Etta! Bring your father a rock about the size of a grapefruit. William, when Etta brings it, put that rock in your groin, and bring your right leg down tight against it. It will help stop the bleeding." He squeezed both sides of the gaping wound together as tight as his two large hands would allow, until the needle and thread arrived for the permanent closure.

Again and again the graying red-haired doctor's muscular arm thrust the needle against the tough hide of his wiry friend with no success. Doc's blue eyes reflected concern and frustration. The flesh refused to give beneath the upholstery needle and blood made Doc's hands slick at the edges of the wound. The white linen thread was no longer white.

"Henry! Get your father's awl." The awl was used to pierce leather and Huckaby was known for his neat leather mending. It had, in fact, mended a harness only yesterday.

The little Mormon had no way of knowing that same awl would be used to brand him for life.

Doc Pollard's mind wandered as he waited for the awl. He hadn't actually practiced medicine since he left Utah soon after the United States went on the gold standard in 1900—when his silver dreams became as empty as his pockets. He had no license to practice medicine in California, so he worked in the fields with the native Californian, William Huckaby. He prayed that his training would now help his friend. The awl was hastily heated in the Huckaby's camp fire. Doc punctured each side of the gash with the awl as perspiration ran down William's face. Doc then easily ran the red-stained linen thread through each hole cinching the edges of the gaping wound.

"You've got the toughest butt in California," the doctor spat.

"Just shut up and keep on patching," William replied. Pain showed on his anguished face. Black, curly hair matted his forehead. His green eyes were squeezed shut.

Both families stood by in silent support, Martha wringing a small rag from her apron pocket. Doc's wife, Roxie Belle, and her six children, huddled close by with the Huckaby family. They each held back tears as their faces grimaced with William's pain. Etta held her mother's shoulders as they flinched with every stitch.

The cooled Indian herb tea was poured into and over the wound. A second warmed cup was thrust into the patient's hands.

"I don't drink tea or coffee, thank you." the worn Mormon said weakly.

Doc gleefully ignored Huckaby's refusal. He finally told William that it was an herb tea, and he could be thankful that it wasn't rotgut whiskey and laudanum.

Doc tore a clean sheet into bandages for dressing and binding the wound. He placed the bandages over a thick coating of Vaseline and several layers of padding. Then Doc wrapped the binding from the back of William's waist over the right buttock, through the legs, around the right thigh and back up to the waist. The binding was then brought around the waist where it was pinned to the beginning. The eight-inch bandage was torn into two four-inch strips down to the pin. The ends were crossed over and under and pulled tight, to stop further tearing of the material. Then Doc brought the end to the front and finally tied it again at the navel.

Doc Pollard sat up and laughed as he straightened his back. "There! That ought to hold your little iron ass in place."

"Little Iron Ass" lost his lacing in due time, and ultimately his reluctance to sit. But he carried Doc Pollard's awl-eyelets' brand and embarrassing nickname for the rest of his life.

PEARLY WHITES

Etta grew to be a striking young woman. Her ebony black hair surrounded her face with soft natural waves. Childish mischief still sparkled behind dark brown eyes. A warm smile showed youthful white teeth as her ready laugh captivated all within hearing. Freshly scrubbed, Etta left a scented trail of light herbs with her nearness. It was rare to find such a sixteen-year-old beauty living in the hot, dry high desert of Moreno Valley in 1901.

Neither Etta nor her younger sister Mattie had little opportunity to meet young men. That changed one day when word got around that a good-looking young man had moved into the little community. Both Etta and Mattie saw him when they went to town to pick up the mail. He stood a little under six-feet, with dark curly hair, blue eyes and beautiful white, even teeth. His rugged tanned face looked freshly shaven, but invitingly soft. A black cap sat jauntily on the back of his head, and a red bandanna around his neck. They talked of nothing else on the way home.

They knew they could not discuss this magnificent find at home. Their parents would see to it that they didn't pick up the mail again if they even guessed that their sixteen and fifteen-year-old daughters were eyeing a handsome young man they knew nothing about. "It's our secret," Etta said.

Mattie was ill the next Friday so Etta was allowed to go to town alone. "Don't walk Ol' Ned too fast and don't lollygag around town. You get back here as soon as you can. I don't want to have to come looking for you."

"Oh, I will, Father. I'll come right home."

The arrow-brush grew tall all around their temporary home close to the canal, and their lean-to could not be seen from the road after the first bend beyond the canal. Etta walked Ol' Ned until she could no longer see her home.

"Come on Ned, we have to get to town as fast as your old legs will carry us," she said as she flung the whip and snapped it far above the old horse's head. The poor old thing took off at an arthritic gallop which raised a cloud of dust that could have been seen as far away as the Salton Sea. Etta was totally unaware of the air-born trail she was leaving. She was on her way to see the handsome young man again. She hoped to get an introduction to him and have a little time to talk before she had to get Ol' Ned home.

Sure enough, there he was at the train station talking with a group of men. *What good luck. There's Fredrick Pollard who works on the railroad. I know I can get him to introduce me.*

"Hello Mr. Pollard," she called. "How's your mother?"
"She's just fine, Miss Etta. How are your family and Mattie in particular?" He smiled as he helped her down from the wagon.

"She's not well at the present. She didn't even feel well enough to come with me to pick up the mail, but I'm sure she'll be up and around soon." They lingered at the edge of the small group of men and Fred introduced her to all the men, including the rakish Ralph Wardlow.

Mr. Wardlow removed his cap and said something about being happy to meet her and even asked if she lived far from town. Soon they were engaged in a friendly exchange. He walked Etta to the post office in the next block. *Things are going well. He is so attentive.* She reluctantly said her goodbyes and turned Ol' Ned toward home.

She walked Ol' Ned all the way home as she day-dreamed of her newly acquired friend, Ralph. *Mattie is going to be so envious.* She smiled to herself and wondered how she could meet him again and promised herself that she would find a way.

Mattie remained ill for a few weeks for which Etta was almost thankful. Not that she wanted Mattie to be truly sick, it was just convenient right at the moment.

Etta was sure that Ralph would ask her to a dance being held on the sixteenth of June. It was just over one month away. She thought of Mattie's anger if she should get the invitation. Oh well, Mattie already had a friend, Fred Pollard. He thought the world of her. So Mattie could just concentrate on Fredrick. "Let's go," she called to Ol' Ned.

Ralph came by the Huckaby place early one Saturday morning with two other men. They were headed over to the Guthrie place. Etta stayed under the arrow-brush lean-to and continued to clear breakfast, but she was close enough to overhear the conversation. Her father was getting along well with the big, good looking fellow. He too, it seemed, was a man of God. They were discussing Ralph's next job. She found that he worked with sheep and was apparently quite good at it. The other two men were bragging to her father on what a "natural" Ralph was and what a quick, clean job he did. The best either of them had seen. Etta was quite impressed.

Mattie was also listening from where she was straightening up the sleeping area beneath the same lean-to. She came over and slapped Etta's shoulder and stuck out her tongue at her. "Smarty," she whispered. Etta returned a smug grin.

"You know, Huckaby, that Ralph here castrated Joe Thompson's entire herd last week. Not one case of infection. I guess that's one advantage of using your teeth. Ralph's teeth are so even that he hardly leaves a scar on the little fellows," one of the men bragged.

"Oh, come on Ben, I'm sure anyone could have done as well," said Ralph graciously.

Etta's mouth dropped and her eyes widened as she turned to Mattie who immediately put her hand over her mouth to stifle her laughter. Both girls were absolutely disgusted. "Are you going to let him kiss you at the dance, Etta?" teased Mattie.

"Shut up Mattie," hissed Etta. "I'm never going out with him. Can you imagine anyone castrating sheep with their mouth? I don't care how good of a job he does."

The girls hurriedly left their living quarters and walked along the canal away from the visitors. Neither of them wanted to be in a position to have to speak to him.

Etta turned to Mattie, "Just think, I could have killed poor Ol' Ned just to meet this stranger with his filthy castrating pearly whites."

TOOTHLESS BOUNDRY

Etta ran out to greet her brother, Henry. Her husband, Walter, had just picked him up at the train station. As they got out of the pickup, Henry kissed her. She loved her older brother, but now in his old age, she did not care for his toothless mouth. She knew he was trying to make her angry when he pressed his mushy, wrinkled, old lips hard against her cheek. He loved to rile her. When he finally released her, he grinned his old "gotcha" smile. *Yuck*!

Walter occupied himself in the garage so the siblings could have time alone.

Henry looked old. His toothless presence slapped Etta with the awareness of their age. They were both old enough to lose all their teeth even though they both still had dark, wavy hair.

"Why didn't you get dentures?" she snapped. Henry knew he was really disturbing her.

"My wallet said that I had a choice to visit you or get dentures. I'd rather see you, Sis." He gave her a big hug and felt her recoil.

"I like seeing you too, Henry."

"I suppose Walter said that you look just marvelous - even without teeth," she said with a tinge of anger. Her irritation with Walter surprised her brother.

He looked at his sister and noticed how young she looked. Her black hair had little grey and her olive skin was smooth as satin with few wrinkles. Their dark brown eyes and rather hooked noses labeled them family. Because he no longer had teeth, he knew that he looked much older. She had always mothered him and there were times when he thought of her as a mother.

"I never did care about my teeth," her brother said. "Remember, I never brushed them when we were kids."

"I don't remember that at all," Etta said.

"I remember it real well. I was out back by the outhouse and I told Mattie I wished that they'd all fall out."

"Remember how Mattie and I always said that no one would ever know if, and when, we had to have false teeth?" Etta asked. "Then, remember how she came right in my house when she got her false teeth, took them out of her mouth and wanted me to look at them? I shut my eyes tight and told her to keep them in her mouth. You must get dentures," she implored.

"What makes you think I want dentures?"

"Henry! Do you want to drive me crazy?"

"Oh, it'll take more than my teeth to do that."

"Please get some dentures. If you only knew how old you look. One can't see anything but your sunken cheeks."

"I'm not going to spend good money for teeth," he said just as firm, but with a twinkle in his soft, brown eyes.

She did not see the twinkle, but saw life changing a little for all of them. *We're all getting old. I'll have Walter speak to him.*

"Are you going to have Walter do your dirty work?" Henry teased when he saw she was lost in thought.

"Don't mock me," Etta said. They had always sparred. There was no anger, but the way they chipped at one another made Walter uncomfortable so he stayed outside.

"Etta, I think Henry looks good," Walter said.

"What about having no teeth makes him look good?"

"His coloring for one thing. Since he's rid of those bad teeth his color is good and his skin coloring looks clearer," Walter said.

He saw her mouth and throat moving with unspoken words. "Where is Henry now?" he wondered out loud.

"I don't know," she said.

"Why do you go on about the inevitable like you do, Etta? Face it. Your big brother is an old, toothless man."

She could not explain to Walter why the toothless gap in Henry's face upset her so. An empty mouth and all it represented lay ahead of her, and she did not want to think about it. Then Henry came along and just shoved it right in her face every time she looked at him.

"It's not the lack of teeth so much. It's the way he looks—so old and he accepts it. He doesn't look like himself and he accepts that too." Her hands played with the corners of her handkerchief in her apron pocket. "Why does he act as though it hasn't happened at all, or that it doesn't bother him?"

"He does look at himself. He has accepted it. You don't accept it, or him. You've always said that Henry was wishy-washy and never knew what he wanted. Well, now he knows what he wants— no dentures. I say leave him alone, and I'm not going to talk to him about it." His gaze lifted toward her but rested finally only on her hands fingering her handkerchief in the yellow and white pocket.

"I will not talk to him about it," Walter said.

Henry stood in front of her. "Before I had my teeth pulled, I sent away for a kit to get dentures made. You made such a fuss, I just had to give you a bad time, Sis. They sent me this black wax to make an imprint of my gums. I thought maybe you'd help me." He grinned at her and revealed his naked gums and tongue.

The events of the day, like a heavy curtain, had seemed to cut her off from her brother and husband. Here was salvation. "Of course I'll help you, Henry. Where are the instructions?" She smiled and took the package from him. "Now then, I'll start the water to boil."

It wasn't hard. They softened the black wax and covered his lower gums with a thick layer, and then Henry pressed his upper gums into the warm, black mass. "Jesus! It smells like shit!" Henry mumbled through closed jaws.

"No matter. Let's get it done," she smiled.

Thank God, thought Etta. At least you can't see the vacant, pink insides of his aging mouth. Of course Henry couldn't talk well since his jaws were sealed shut for thirty minutes, but she smiled and thought how well everything was working out. She smoothed her apron over her slight frame.

"All right, Henry, it's time. Be careful. Don't wiggle your jaws. Just pull them slowly and steadily apart...that's it. Come on. Pull!"

Henry's face was contorted and as he pulled, his muffled curses filled the air. His red neck depicted either rage or strain. Either way, it was not a pretty sight or sound.

Etta tried pouring cold water on the wax, but other than almost drowning Henry, had no success. "Oh, what to do! What to do!" Etta cried. She turned and ran outside to find Walter.

Walter, who knew nothing of their adventure until that moment, followed Etta back into the kitchen with a quizzical look on his face. He took one look at Henry's distorted face, heard his jumbled curses, smelled the vile black wax, and became one big ball of laughter. Neither Henry nor Etta could yet find the humor in the situation.

"You-son-of-a-bitch," came out surprisingly clear as Henry glared at Walter's uncontrollable laughter.

Walter put his hands on Henry's shoulders, still laughing, his large belly dancing and trying to talk at the same time. Finally he got out that he (Henry) would be all right. "I'll get that crap off your gums. You should try brushing your teeth more often."

"What-er-ya-gonna-do?"

"Don't you worry. Just lay down on your back here on the kitchen floor while I go out for my tools."

By that time every kid in the house was in the kitchen to watch Uncle Henry get his gums knocked out by Grandpa.

Small and wiry at five feet, seven inches, Henry meekly obeyed. Burly, six feet, 200 pound, Walter soon straddled his waist with a tap hammer and small chisel in hand.

A few of Grandma's roomers came in to witness this operation and every one of them were giggling and whispering.

"What-er-ya-gonna-do?" Henry repeated, only louder.

"Just relax. I'm going to just tap this black crap a little, and it's going to fall right off. Pull your lips back." Walter hesitated when a new round of laughter hit him.

Henry's curses could still be heard as Walter tapped away between peals of laughter. By that time Etta was beyond worry and was also enjoying Henry's plight. Henry's eyes widened to an all-time record and his small frame poured sweat. His collarless shirt was wet to the waist. The laughing bear hanging over him was not a cooling or reassuring experience.

"God-damn-it, Walter, stop laughing and hurry up. Pay attention to what you're doin'. These are my gums your foolin' around with," Henry mumbled. With that, Walter hit a little harder and the black wax broke apart. Henry's jaws flew open and the chisel almost entered his throat.

Etta and Walter helped him up. Henry cursed and spit black chips with everyone laughing and congratulating them. In the next few days the black wax began to peel off. Henry swore that he would never buy dentures—never.

Henry's visit was much shorter than his usual stay. He was the butt of many jibes about the way he gummed morsels into oblivion and how he "saucered and blowed" his coffee. He felt he could not eat and carry on a conversation, especially if he was pleasant and smiled. Etta silently prayed that she would never let anyone see her if she lost all her teeth.

"Henry, please come back soon. We had such a good time."

"Sis, I know everyone wound up enjoying my empty mouth. I earned the loss of every one of my teeth. It wasn't easy looking into the mirror at first. I know I remind you of what's going to happen to you. But my being fancy with etiquette and keeping my mouth shut aren't going to change my looks, your age, or bring back my teeth. Every one of us is aging and stuck with it. So just let me be."

She saw the hurt look on Henry's face. What if their positions were reversed? Henry would never call her an old woman.

Etta threw her arms around Henry's neck and said, "Oh, Henry, I'm so sorry. You're right. We are at an age where family should see more, not less of one another. Teeth or no teeth, you're still my pain-in the-behind brother and I love you. Besides, as mother used to say, 'It will never be noticed on a galloping horse a mile away.'"

NINE GENERATIONS AT KING'S RIVER

Last week I introduced my four oldest great-grandchildren to their local ancestors. We drove through Centerville, California to The Old Akers Cemetery. Some of our family members arrived at Kings River in Fresno County about 1853. They arrived in oxen-drawn covered wagons. Those same pioneers are now buried in what was, at one time, their own front yard.

My last visit to the cemetery was nine years ago. Skyler, my oldest and only great-granddaughter, was less than a year old on that visit. It had looked unkempt with large weeds and broken headstones scattered beneath the old oaks. I hoped this small, hallowed space would look more cared for during this visit. I wanted my little descendants to feel respect for the resting place of these brave, early settlers.

With interruptions and constant questions, I told them of the long-ago wagon trip which began in Kentucky and slowly moved toward Texas and ultimately California. I pointed out that Delilah Miller Akers left Texas for California in 1852. She traveled with a very large wagon train which included many of her relatives. Nine of her twelve children still lived at home, and she brought all of them with her. Her husband, Henry Akers, was against the move and did not accompany her on the trip. He did not follow his family until after August 1875.

Skyler seemed to realize many of the problems of such a trip and expressed awe over Delilah's bravery.

One of those children making the trip with Delilah was my great-grandfather's mother, Margie Ann Akers Huckaby. I explained the nine generations between Delilah and each of my great-grandchildren by the name and relationship of each generation.

"One of Delilah's children, who made the trip with Delilah, married David Huckaby when she grew up. Their oldest child was William Henry Huckaby. He married Martha Ann Casteel. Their third child was Etta May Huckaby who married Walter Doyle Pollard. Etta and Walter Pollard were my grandma and grandpa. They had my mother, Mildred Alta Pollard, and she married my father, Everett Thurlow Enloe. I was their oldest child, and I, Winnie May Enloe, married Arnold Walter Furrer. I had your grandmother, Theresa Ann Furrer. When she married Dayne Mortensen, she gave birth to Heather and Danielle Mortensen. Heather had Skyler, Bryce and Chase. Danielle had Jake."

As I pointed to each of them, I said, "See how each of you have the blood and traits of all those who came before you?"

I told the kids they would see where Delilah, their oldest ancestor, was buried here in Aker's Cemetery.

"Uh huh," one of them replied with boredom.

The fence around the small graveyard had been fixed, but as we drew alongside, I could see there were far fewer headstones standing than at my last visit. Many partial headstones were scattered around with bases still in the ground but not associated with a headstone. The second I stopped the car in the shade, kids erupted from all four doors.

"Stop! We go in as a group. Be quiet! Remember this is a cemetery. Do you hear me? There may be snakes."

Five year old Jake raced back and asked, "Why are you yelling, Grandma? You said to be quiet."

By this time all four were milling around me. "This is a very special place. These people were related to you. Look at all the names on this large plaque. Do you understand that they are buried here in this ground?"

"Yeah! Let's go find them," yelled six year old Bryce, already in flight. This naturally pulled the two five year olds into his wake. Chase, the mouth, rated highest on the decibel scale.

Skyler, who is ten turning thirty, and I, followed them toward what I knew was Delilah's headstone. Skyler asked quietly as she took my hand, "Grandma, who takes care of these people?"

"I don't know, hon. They started a community here and learned to depend on each other so they all deserved to spend eternity together. I think this entire community tries to care for them. Wouldn't you, if we lived closer?"

"Can we come back and maybe help clean it up?"

"I'll try to find out who owns the ground now." I squeezed her hand.

As we got to Delilah's stone, the boys were already giving it the once over. Bryce let us know that there were different names on each side of the stone. I pointed out that one side was my Great-Great-Grandmother's stone, Margie Akers Huckaby, Delilah's daughter. I felt their change immediately. They each stopped and smiled up at me. I heard small utterances as their hands seem to pet the stone. The stone belonged to them now. "Who's this one?" And before I could answer, the fourth side was pointed to. "Who's this?'

"Delilah's husband, Henry Akers, and another daughter, Mrs. Elizabeth Howard," I answered. They continued to love the stone.

Skyler asked if they placed the stone to each person's head. Before I could answer Bryce laughingly said, "That would make an x." Then they all became concerned with standing on the graves.

I told them that the stones had been moved so we had no way of knowing just where each person was actually buried. "They know we are here, and I think they all like to have us come and visit. That's the important thing."

Chase looked up at me and asked, "Are we supposed to love 'um?"

"We should appreciate what they went through for us. If they hadn't had the courage to bring their family all the way to California in a covered wagon, you and I wouldn't be here. Do you think they were brave?"

They each agreed they loved every one of these ancestors and thought they were all brave. They asked me if I knew them and if I loved them. "I wasn't born when they lived here, so I never met them. But from what I've head of them, I'm proud we have their blood and genes in our bodies. Yes, I love each one of them and I'm sorry I never met them."

We walked over to what I thought was the "Akers' marrying tree." I was told it was still standing at the side of the road a short distance from the cemetery. Long ago it stood in Delilah's front yard. It was a family tradition to be married beneath its branches. "Kids, Margie Akers married David Huckaby under this old tree."

At last I heard the question I knew was coming, "Were there Indians?" asked Jake. The answer to his question occupied us throughout the drive north and east, where we stopped to eat our picnic lunch at Winton County Park.

I explained that all of the wagon people were thankful to the Pima Indians in Arizona for saving the entire wagon train from starvation on their journey from Texas. The Indians taught the people to find unfamiliar food and liquid in the arid landscape. This knowledge gave the travelers security to travel without fear of running low on food again.

The Indians were treated with respect and taught to use tools in ways which made their lives easier. By helping each another, the two groups became friends. The Indian people wanted the people from the wagon train to stay in Arizona and live with them.

During their lifetimes many trips were made by both parties to and from Yuma. Each group of friends continued to keep in touch over many generations. I explained that the Indian's real name was one I couldn't pronounce, spelled Akicrnel O'odharn. It meant *river people.*

The kids threw rocks into the Kings River for awhile after lunch and continued to come back to me with more questions. The ancestors were still in their hearts, but their questions told me they still didn't understand their relationship with the old cemetery. But I think it was a day well spent. I feel the spirits in that hallowed ground were pleased to hear young voices ringing out and small feet tromping on their hardened roofs. I think hearts met and after all, it was their first introduction.

THE DESTRUCTION OF THE *U.S.S. PHILADELPHIA*
By John Noel

Beneath a silver Mediterranean moon, the *Mastico* sailed into the pirate stronghold of Tripoli. Light February breezes ruffled the sails as the little ship hissed through the waves.

Two men stood near the wheel. One was Lt. Stephen Decatur of the United States Navy. The other was a pilot who knew the harbor and the Arabic language.

Ahead, a fortress loomed menacingly against the lights of the city. Somewhere inside was the pasha, a ruler who made piracy Tripoli's national pastime. He demanded protection money from the United States. When President Thomas Jefferson refused to pay, the pasha brazenly declared war. The Tripolitan pirates attacked American ships. The captured crew members were held for ransom or sold into slavery. To be caught in the pasha's own harbor would mean certain death.

The young lieutenant calmly ignored the cannons bristling from the pasha's fort and scanned the darkened harbor. Suddenly he nudged the pilot and pointed. Straight ahead, resting at anchor, lay a huge warship. It was the pride of the American fleet, the 36-gun frigate *U.S.S. Philadelphia.*

A few months earlier, on October 31, 1803, the *Philadelphia* had run aground near the North African coast. When the pasha's corsairs saw that the mighty frigate was helpless, they quickly surrounded it with gunboats. The captain surrendered the ship and its crew of over 300.

44

The pasha's men managed to refloat the *Philadelphia* and towed it to Tripoli. There they set about turning it into the most powerful pirate ship that ever sailed the seas. Decatur's mission was to make sure that would never happen.

With 75 volunteers, Decatur boarded the *Mastico*, a captured priate ship, and set off for Tripoli. The voyage was dangerous. The Americans were tossed by violent storms. They were seasick, wet and cold. Their salt pork went bad, and they survived on bread and water.

Nearing their destination, they carefully picked their way through the same uncharted reefs that had grabbed the *Philadelphia*. Twice the ship approached Tripoli only to be driven back by changes in the wind.

Finally, on the night of February 16, 1804, the *Mastico* entered the enemy harbor. The men aboard probably wished they were back at sea. Tripoli was home port to as many as 25,000 pirates. A score of armed ships lay anchored nearby. The *Philadelphia* itself was occupied by a full crew. Its big guns were loaded with double shot.

Into this deadly trap Decatur and his men boldly sailed. Their weapons were swords, for the use of guns would alert the entire harbor. Their protection was disguise. The *Mastico* was of Arab design, and the few sailors on deck wore Arab clothing. The other American sailors hid as the *Mastico* made her perilous run.

About ten o'clock, the *Mastico* came within hailing distance of the frigate. A pirate lookout shouted a challenge. "Who are you?" he demanded.

"We are a Maltese ship," the pilot called back. "Our anchors have been lost. Can you help us?"

The ruse brought the Americans a few precious minutes as they edged ever closer. Just as the *Mastico* reached the *Philadelphia*, however, a pirate sounded the alarm. "Americanos!" he cried.

Decatur did not hesitate. "Board!" he yelled.

Steel flashing in the moonlight, the Americans swarmed onto the *Philadelphia*. The surprised pirates panicked. Many of them jumped overboard. Others ran below to hide. In just ten minutes, Americans were once again in control of the *Philadelphia*.

There was no chance of getting the *Philadelphia* out of the harbor, so the men raced about the vessel setting fires. As smoke began pouring from the hold, they scrambled back to the *Mastico*. Decatur, the last to leave, jumped into the rigging as the *Mastico* pulled away.

Even then, the Americans were hardly out of danger. The raging fire lit up the harbor for the pirate gunners in the fortress. Shot flew thick and fast around the fleeing boat. Miraculously, there were no direct hits. Not one American was lost that night.

Beyond the range of pirate guns at last, the exhausted sailors rested and watched the fiery spectacle. Tongues of orange flame leaped from the *Philadelphia*'s portholes. Burning sails and rigging showered sparks everywhere. Overheated cannons discharged with thunderous booms. The inferno cast a flickering glare upon the enraged pasha's fortress.

Finally, a terrific explosion shook the entire harbor. Flaming fragments blasted into the night sky like fireworks in a final, awesome display. The once-proud *Philadelphia* was no more.

Bibliography
Blasingame, Wyatt. Stephen Decatur. Champaign, IL: Garrard Publishing, 1964
Chapell, Howard I. The History of the American Sailing Navy. New York: Bonanza Books, 1949.
Cross, Wilbur. Naval Battles and Heroes. New York: American Heritage, 1960.

Foner, Eric and Garraty, John, editors. <u>The Reader's Companion to American History</u>. Boston: Houghton, Mifflin, 1991.

Forester, C.S. "Bloodshed at Dawn." Article in *American Heritage,* October 1964.

Lodge, Henry Cabot. <u>Hero Tales from American History</u>. Quoted in *American Heritage*, June 1967.

Maclay, Edgar Stanton. <u>A History of the United States Navy</u>. New York: D. Appleton and Co., 1898.

Rubel, David. <u>Encyclopedia of the Presidents and Their Times</u>. New York: Scholastic, Inc. 1994.

WILD BILL AND POKER DUMMY
By John Noel

My most embarrassing moment was rooted in a holiday tradition—the annual Christmas Poker Game at the in-laws' house.

Not knowing much about poker, I avoided the game for years, but last year I was determined to play. I even bought *Poker for Dummies* so I could learn the basics.

As Christmas Day neared, there were no images of sugar plums dancing in my head. Nope, I was conjuring up images of Wild Bill Hickock, Bret Maverick, Rooster Cogburn and Jesse James sitting in a smoke-filled saloon, warily eyeing each other over their cards.

Even the names of the various poker games sounded exciting: Five Card Stud, Spit in the Ocean, Texas Hold 'Em. Poker is a man's world. Kids and womenfolk take cover! Put a head on that beer, barkeep! Light up them stogies, boys! Deal 'em, pilgrim.

Finally, there I was, sitting at the big table in the garage with the menfolk of the family. I bought ten dollars' worth of chips and practiced my poker face as Mark, the first dealer, shuffled the cards. Joey cut the deck and Mark announced his game of choice.

"OK, we're playing . . . fivecarddrawwithdeuceswildbutonlyasacesandinflushes," he said. "Ready?"

"Ummm, no," I said uncertainly. Speaking of flushes, I was already heading down the toilet. I had absolutely no idea what Mark was talking about.

Patiently, but with an ever-so-slightly-pained expression, Mark explained the rules for this hand. I still had no idea what he was talking about. But I did what any self-respecting gambler would do, I bluffed.

"All right, sounds good," I mumbled.

Mark dealt. We played. I lost.

The next hand didn't go any better. "Ante up, boys," Anthony said as the cards whirred in his hands. "We're playing Sevencardstuflastcarddownwithwildladies!"

"Cool!" everyone said.

"Huh?" I said.

Again they explained. I nodded. We played. I lost.

At that point I was hoping for aces and eights, the Dead Man's Hand, so that maybe someone would shoot me like they did poor Wild Bill back in Deadwood. Except that I felt more like Howdy Doody than Wild Bill.

That's pretty much the way it went. Hand after hand of poker variations I had never heard of. Hand after hand my pile of chips dwindled. The only flushes I got were on my face when I sprayed the cards while shuffling or forgot to ante.

Finally, mercifully, my last poker chip plinked into Arnie's pot at the end of a game of . . .

Corcorantrashwithoneeyedjacksandredeightswildinpairs.

"Well, that cleans me out," I said. "Thanks for the game."

I got up from the table, gracefully bumping my knee and spilling Joey's beer. Mumbling apologies, I limped back into the house to join the womenfolk and young 'uns.

Like any good cowboy, however, I was soon back in the saddle. Just an hour later I was playing cards again, and this time I was winning and winning big.

I glared over my hand at my four-year-old nephew, Jeff, who was holding his jumbled cards way out where I could see everything he had.

"You gots any frees?" he asked.

"Sorry pardner," I said. "Go fish!"

John Noel

Eleven-One
By John Noel

When bleary-eyed bats flutter into the wall
Trying to find their cave
And the mummy's feeling a bit unwrapped
While Drac's passed out in his grave

When monsters, snoring like thunder
Lie covered with morning dew
And the witches are all hung over
From drinking the dregs of their brew

When skeletons search for fingers and ribs
Lost in the rattle and roll,
And goblins and ghouls have fallen asleep
Under the bridge with the troll

When the werewolf's beard has gone from his chin
And the gremlin's too tired to remember
When all of the ghosts have faded away
Then you know it's the first of November

When Jack O'Lantern's lost his grin
And black cats strike no fear,
When the only thing groaning's a candy-stained kid
Then Halloween's gone for a year

A Hag's Demise
By John Noel

Over a graveyard on Halloween Night,
An old witch zoomed on her broom.
Her yearly flight was meant to spread fright,
But instead she met her doom.

She zigged, she zagged, she swooped and then
That showoff soared and slashed.
She stood on the handle hanging ten,
And into a big oak she smashed.

Dangling there with her slimy hair
Tangled all up in the twigs,
She said some words that you won't dare
to say until you're big.

Oh the werewolves howled and the bats all hid,
And the mummy crept home to her crypt.
Ol' Drac peeked out from his coffin lid,
Then under his covers he slipped.

There she hung all through the night
Until the sun started to rise.
The dawning light ended the fright
As it sizzled the hag's green eyes.

She moaned and she groaned, but 'twas no use,
And she screamed till her face turned red.
She squirmed like a worm, but she couldn't get loose.
And by morning she was dead.

WordJam
By John Noel

I love the crush of traffic
On my computer screen

Cursor blinking
Words buzzing
Sentences flowing
Paragraphs heaving
New ideas merge
Insert! Insert!
Tired phrases chug to the off-ramps
Highlight and delete!

The writing comes to life
Breathing
Pulsing
Driving

Commas and periods jump into the gaps
As my fingertips clack out a rhythm —
Then
Comes
A
Trafficjamslowdowntrafficjamtraffictrafficstopjamtrafficjam
And
I
Wait   wait   wait   wait
For   the   words   to   move   again …

S-Words
By John Noel

One is
Easy to say
Slips out sometimes
even when it shouldn't

The other is
hard to say.
Clogs the throat sometimes,
even when it shouldn't.

John Noel

Lost loves …
Secret haunting ghosts
You/I/we/all have
You/I/we/all are

There are miles/years between my/your/our hearts
Not short miles
Not light years…
Heavy years filling in the time/space between you/me/us

Somewhere standing in a kitchen
Family chattering about her
Glancing at the darkened window she sees her now reflection
Never imagining her younger reflection visible to me
Through myriad nights
Through long miles
Through heavy years

I wonder if she even knows she's my lost love

Am I hers? I don't know.
And she is not here to ask.
We/us/together flashed brightly/quickly
Our eternity did not last forever
Slowly she/me/we/us/together became

She
          And
                    I

Lost loves
Nothing but ghosts
Fading in the gray attics of my/your/all hearts.

By John Noel

THE HEADGATE
By
Mary Martin Benton

Crimson rays of early sunlight streaked over the nearby Sierra when we arrived at the tomato fields. Rusty cars and dented trucks lined the edge of the field next to a large canal on the eastern edge of California's San Joaquin Valley. The air was crisp with morning dew, and I pulled my worn sweater closer around me.

Daddy stepped from our old '37 Plymouth and yawned. "Looks like a good crew showed up today," he said to Mama and Aunt Teresa.

Aunt Teresa, Mama's younger sister, was staying with us for a while. She was tying her hair up with an orange- colored bandana as Mama rummaged around in the trunk of our sedan.

"Do you see Clyde?" Aunt Teresa asked Daddy.

"What you see in that loafer is beyond me," Daddy retorted. "You just left one bum, now you're making eyes at another one. Why don't you set your sights a little higher? Now, old Bob Bateman's one good eye has been wandering all over you. He might be missing a few teeth and have a gimpy leg, but at least he has his own land. Damn, girl. Make hay while the sun shines. You won't have your good looks forever."

Aunt Teresa laughed. "Why Leroy, Old Bob wouldn't last the night with me. I'd be a widow before the ink dried on the marriage license."

"Honey, that's the plan," Daddy drawled slowly.

Mama pulled out an old, patchwork quilt made from worn overalls and handed it to my sister, Ima Jean. "Spread this out under that cottonwood tree by the canal bank," she instructed her. "You and Bernadette can play there."

Since I was older than Ima Jean, Mama handed me the heavy ice cooler to carry. "You make sure this stays in the shade, Bernadette. I don't want to be eating spoiled sandwiches for lunch."

I yes-mam'ed her and trudged through the soft dirt to where Ima Jean had spread out the quilt. After placing the cooler under an elderberry bush, I sat down on the quilt with Ima Jean. We were both barefoot and my feet were getting cold. I pulled my knees up and tried to cover my feet by stretching my sweater over them. Ima Jean lay down and curled up, pulling the edge of the quilt over her. I watched as Mama and Daddy and Aunt Teresa gathered up their picking buckets and walked to the field with the rest of the crew.

Daddy gave Aunt Teresa a hard time now and then, but I think she enjoyed his teasing. I was glad she was staying with us. She was my favorite aunt.

Their voices faded and the pails on the metal buckets clanged in the morning air as they and the pickers disappeared into the staked rows of tall tomato vines. A dove mourned softly in the branches of the cottonwood above me, and I could hear the call of a quail in the distance. Daddy said they were calling the other quails and inviting them to "Sit-right-here." As the quietness settled around me, I became aware of the distant roar of water.

I prodded my sister with one foot. "Come on, Ima Jean. Let's go see what's making that sound." I scrambled up the embankment of the canal like a mountain goat while Ima Jean followed more slowly. "Wow," I exclaimed as I stood on top of the canal bank and eyed the rolling water. "That looks deep."

About a hundred feet up the canal bank was a headgate. Water spilling over the boards in the dam made the roaring sound. "Hey," I called down to Ima Jean. "I see what's making that noise. Hurry up. You're as slow as Old Granny Grunt."

It sounded like she mumbled, "Shut up," to me, but then Ima Jean always *was* a grouch in the mornings.

I hurried to the headgate and was mesmerized by the water as it poured over the heavy planks. A wide piece of lumber spanned the top of the weir. Tentatively, I placed one foot on the narrow footbridge. Ima Jean walked up behind me. I could barely hear her over the noise of the water.

"You better not, Bernadette. Mama said we were to play under the tree."

"Yeah, but she didn't say that we *couldn't* play on the headgate," I said with all the defiance my ten-year old voice could muster.

Bravely, I stepped onto the narrow footbridge. The rush I felt as I crossed over the dangerous waterway made me giddy. I flapped my elbows and did a rooster strut as I walked back across the top of the dam.

"You're a complete idiot," Ima Jean shouted at me. She had her arms crossed over her chest and was glaring at me.

"Just because you're a big sissy-fart, doesn't mean I am," I said. I stepped off the plank and onto the cement pillar that supported it. I turned and wiggled my butt at her. "Sissy-fart, sissy-fart," I chanted. That's when I felt her hands hit my behind, shoving me forward. My body was suspended in midair for only a moment before I hit the churning water.

It felt like ice. It turned and rolled me like a pair of overalls in a giant washing machine. I squeezed my eyes shut and held my breath as I flailed and kicked against the dark, swirling water. My hands banged against the rocks and mud that lined the bottom of the canal. One foot touched a rock and I pushed against it, propelling myself upward. My head popped out of the water and I quickly pulled the misty air into my starving lungs. I opened my eyes and caught a glimpse of Ima Jean. She was standing rock-still on the canal bank, staring at me with a look of frozen horror on her face.

The weight of the thrashing water pushed against my arms. I struggled to pull them up and into a position where I could keep myself afloat. The water spilling over the weir rained down on me. I gulped another mouthful of air as water boiled over my head. An invisible force sucked at my body, pulling me under. Instinct took control. *Find the bottom and push yourself up.* The churning water tumbled me forward, rolling me over and over. My hands hit the bottom again and I could feel the sandy mud. I dug my fingers into the silt, stopping my somersaults for a moment. Shoving my feet downward, I kicked hard. My chest was burning something fierce when the fresh air rushed across my face. The foaming water from the spillway roared behind me as I swirled and bobbed downstream. Tilting my head back, I gasped for air and inhaled the muddy water. Choking and coughing, I fought to keep my head above the cold current.

A scrub willow grew next to the bank, its branches dipping low into the water. I dog-paddled toward it. Grasping at the narrow leaves, my hand caught a thin branch. I held on tightly and saw Ima Jean racing down the canal bank toward me. Her mouth was open and I could tell she was screaming something, but I couldn't hear her.

The branch snapped. Once again I was spinning in the water as the current carried me away from the bank and Ima Jean.

Then I saw Mama and Aunt Teresa. They were both running down the canal bank. Mama's face was grim and determined. They both wore loose-fitting jeans and men's denim work shirts. Somewhere along the way they had lost the large, straw hats they wore in the field.

Aunt Teresa easily outran Mama. I saw her as she slid down the embankment ahead of me. Her hand was reaching for me and I heard her shout. "Grab my hand, Bernadette! Over here, baby doll!"

Water washed over my face as I slipped beneath the surface. My hand brushed against hers. I wiggled my fingers and felt her strong grip close around them. From under the water I could see Aunt Teresa's blurry body as she plunged into the canal. The large trousers ballooned up around her legs and the work shirt lifted and swirled in the current. I reached for that swirling shirt, caught it, and twisted my fingers into the fabric. I felt her hands under me, lifting me up and pushing me toward the bank. Rough, calloused hands grabbed my arms and pulled me up the muddy bank.

My eyes stung and I was shivering. Water and bile scalded my mouth as the liquid spewed out and into the dirt. I was lying on my stomach on the canal bank, my cheek flat against the ground. I couldn't remember exactly how I got there, or how long it had been, but the hot dirt felt good against my body. I wanted to roll in it, covering myself with its dry, powdery hotness.

Above the roar in my head Aunt Teresa's voice was a soft whisper. "Come on, sweetie. Take a breath." Forceful hands pressed against my back and I realized Mama was straddling me, bearing down on my ribcage, pushing the muddy canal water from my lungs. I wished she wouldn't push so hard. My chest hurt, my head hurt and everything looked hazy. A jumble of blurred faces crowded around me, each offering advice. Aunt Teresa's soft drawl rose above the babble as she spoke to Mama.

"She's okay now, Lynette. No need you trying to get her to puke out any more water. She'll be fine."

But Mama just kept on pushing. Lordy, I sure wished she would listen to Aunt Teresa.

The next thing I knew Daddy was there. He started cussing like he always does, making it all Mama's fault for letting me and Ima Jean play on the headgate. I wanted to explain to him that it wasn't Mama's fault and it wasn't Ima Jean's fault. It was mine. But the more I tried to talk, the more dirt got inside my mouth and gritted between my teeth.

Mama got up and walked down the canal bank. She stood quietly, staring down at the rolling water. I could tell she was crying by the way she rubbed her face with both hands. Mama never made a noise when she cried. But you knew. A lady from the field walked over and put her arm around Mama.

Daddy bent over me, muttering more cuss words as he scooped me up. Several of the men from the picking crew stood in a tight knot on the canal bank. Daddy's voice was raspy as he spoke to them. "Soon as I run the family home, I'll be back."

It had been a long while since Daddy carried me, but I remembered the smell of his closeness. It was a mixture of sweat and tobacco. He always carried a can of Prince Albert in his shirt pocket along with all his fixings. Daddy is a big man and he didn't carry me none too gently. I tried to tell him I could walk, but he wouldn't listen. He just kept on taking those big, long strides of his, holding me out in front of him like I'm a sacrificial lamb or an offering of some such.

I could see Mama walking behind us. Mama had her hands clasped in front of her, rubbing them together. I couldn't see Aunt

Teresa, but I could hear her voice as she tried to calm Mama down. Ima Jean lagged behind them, alternating between stumbling over furrows and cat-walking the bank of a small irrigation ditch.

When we got to the car Daddy yelled at Ima Jean to open the damn door. She scurried around us and yanked the back door open. Daddy sat me in the back seat and then eased me over so I could lie on my side. I felt Aunt Teresa slide in against me and sit on the edge of the cushion beside me. Mama made Ima Jean sit up front with her and Daddy.

Daddy didn't waste much time getting us home. I was glad. I wanted to tell Ima Jean that I was sorry I had called her a sissy-fart. I wanted to tell her that I was all right. But mostly I wanted to sleep.

Aunt Teresa's presence next to me was a comfort. I longed to sit up and hug her.

"Feeling better, sugar?" I heard her ask.

I tried to tell her thank you for saving me, but the words wouldn't form in my head. Then I heard Daddy again. He never could talk without cussing and he was directing it at Mama like always. I looked at the back of Mama's head. She'd shifted her body and was staring out the window at the dusty fields and I knew she was still crying.

Aunt Teresa's soft voice bordered on scolding. "No use your cussing, Leroy. Bernadette is fine. You can cuss all you want, but it doesn't undo what's already been done. Besides, all you're doing is upsetting Lynette." But Daddy didn't listen and just kept on cussing.

When we got home, Daddy pulled me from the car and carried me inside. I would rather have walked, but he picked me up before I could say anything. The screen door banged against the wall when Daddy kicked it open with his boot. He carried me through the house and onto the back-screened porch. This was where Ima Jean and I slept. We liked it out there. It was cool in the summer and we could listen to the night sounds and tell each other secrets. The beds were soft with feather ticking. Big, goose-down pillows lay plumped against the painted iron-rail headboards.

Daddy laid me on my bed. Ima Jean flopped down on hers and stared at me. Tears had paved runways through the dust on her round cheeks. I was worried about her. She shouldn't have been sitting on her bed. Once our beds were made, we were never allowed to sit or lie on them until it was bedtime.

But here I was, laid out on my bed like a fairy princess, my clothes drenching and staining the pink chenille bedspread. Panic set in about then. The bedspread would be ruined. Mama had ordered them special for Ima Jean's and my Christmas presents from the Sears and Roebuck catalogue. I almost told Ima Jean to get up or Mama was going to be mad. But I knew Mama had already seen her sitting there and didn't say anything, so I let it go.

Aunt Teresa was there next to Ima Jean. My eyesight was still a bit blurry, but I could see her lean over and kiss Ima Jean gently on the cheek, then brush her hand over Ima Jean's mussed hair. "Don't be so glum, sweetie," I heard her say. "Bernadette is safe. No need to beat yourself up over this." But Ima Jean only slumped lower on the bed and didn't pay her no mind. Aunt Teresa turned to me, smiled and winked.

Mama come in then with a washbasin of warm water and some washcloths. She stripped my wet clothes off and began to wash me. I guess she thought I was bruised up some 'cause she wasn't as rough with me as she used to be. I remember when I was little, Mama would near scrub the hide off when she gave me a bath. "Bernadette," she would say, "your knees and face look like you've been out pecking with the chickens!"

Mama finished washing me and then worked the bedspread out from underneath. She turned to the old bureau that stood against the wall and pulled out my favorite nightgown. It was the sleeveless one, made of soft, flour-sack cotton with large blue and white daises printed on it. Mama lifted my head and slid the gown over my wet hair. Picking up each of my arms, she carefully pulled them through the armholes and worked the gown down over my body. She pulled the sheet up to my chin, folded it down, and placed my arms on top.

Mama leaned over me and I could smell the pungent vinegar-like scent of tomato vines fused into her clothes. She brushed a worn hand against my cheek. "Sleep, dear baby," she said softly.

I thought that was a good idea, seeing as how tired I was. In fact, I must have slept for a month of Tuesdays.

When I awoke, I apologized to Ima Jean right off. Since I had my voice back, I figured I would also apologize to Aunt Teresa. I asked Mama where she was. A painful look came over Mama's face. "Bernadette," she said, "your Aunt Teresa drowned."

"What! When?" I asked, not sure how long I had been asleep.

Mama's face twisted up and tears came to her eyes. She started shaking her head. "You poor child, you don't remember." Her voice was soft, like she thought I was addled.

"Remember what?" I ask, turning to Ima Jean. But Ima Jean began to bawl and ran out of the room.

Mama took a deep breath and patted me on the head. "You rest Bernadette, I have a lot of things that need tending to."

"No!" I shouted. "You're wrong. Aunt Teresa didn't drown. She's here, in the house. I saw her."

Mama's face tells me I'm trying her patience. "You were only hallucinating, Bernadette."

My head fell back on the pillow. Is it true, I wondered? But if it *is* so, why was Mama being so nice to me? Why wasn't Daddy strapping me good? I felt sick. A sickness that filled me with dread and weighed my body down like heavy clay.

The next few days passed in a daze of bewilderment. I kept looking for Aunt Teresa. I knew she was somewhere close, hiding, playing one of her pranks. I needed to find her. I wanted to apologize to her and laugh with her when we told Mama it was all a joke.

I thought Aunt Teresa was carrying things too far when they held a funeral for her. She looked so beautiful lying in the casket. Couldn't they see she was all right? I just knew she would sit up in the middle of Pastor Klint's big eulogy and laugh and say, "Got you all good this time!"

Now I must confess, Daddy was a bit rough on me when I started yelling at the cemetery about not putting her in the ground, that she wasn't dead. He hustled me back to the car and shook me until my teeth rattled.

"Bernadette," he said through gritted teeth, "get it through your thick skull that Teresa's dead and none of your pretending and silliness will bring her back." He took a deep breath and pushed his hat back. "For God's sake, even Ima Jean knows better than to act like your acting."

That gave me an idea. Aunt Teresa had kissed Ima Jean on the cheek the night they were sitting on the bed together. Surely Ima Jean would remember. I waited until night and we were alone out in the sleeping porch. I asked her plain-like if she remembered it. I heard her start to breathe heavy and knew I shouldn't have brought it up. Her words were almost indiscernible, muffled like they were with all her sobbing.

"Bernadette," she finally managed, "I called you an idiot that day because you are. No, Aunt Teresa wasn't on the bed with me and I didn't see or feel anything. But I wish she had been and it was *you* that had drowned!"

Her words cut into me like a rusty knife. I rolled over and curled into a ball. *She wasn't the only one that wished it had been me who had drowned.*

After that night, guilt became part of my persona. I wore it like a spiked chain of penance. Rarely laughing, I performed my chores with quiet obedience. I strived to be the perfect child. I owed it to Mama and Daddy and Ima Jean.

*****

The years passed and Ima Jean did lighten up on me. Mama and Daddy never spoke about Aunt Teresa's death. In fact, they rarely spoke to each other at all and Daddy began to smell more like whiskey than tobacco.

For me, winters passed in muffled tule fog. Summers were a blur of blistering heat and flat, white skies. I wished desperately for someone to talk with about Aunt Teresa. To reminisce about her wonderful smile, her soft drawl and loving heart. In desperation, I asked Ima Jean what she remembered about that day. She shook her head and told me she could barely recall it.

The summer I turned fifteen I began helping Mama and Daddy in the fields picking tomatoes. It was a day similar to the day of Aunt Teresa's drowning. The field boss had blown a whistle to signify it was lunchtime. It had been a hard day for me. I had bruised a number of large tomatoes by holding them too tight when I cut them from the vine. Daddy didn't hold back any when he lit into me. I took the sandwich Mama offered, and wanting to put some distance between myself and Daddy, I walked down to the canal.

As I approached the headgate, I hesitated. I hadn't been back to the site since the drowning. The willows on each side of the weir had grown tall. Their swaying limbs created a shaded canopy over the headgate. Under the trees, the layers of decomposing leaves and debris gave off a sweet, earthy smell. I stepped up on the cement pillar and could hear Ima Jean's words echo in my mind. *"You better not, Bernadette."*

My chest constricted and my heart beat faster as I placed one foot on the wide span of lumber that lay across the top of the headgate. The spray from the churning water sifted against my face. It was cool and inviting. I moved my other foot up and inched along the board to the center of the canal. I sat down, and after removing my shoes and socks, rolled the legs of my jeans up. My legs dangled from the weir and I stared at the rolling water. It would be easy to fall forward, no more looks of pity, no more guilt.

A soft, cool breeze kicked up and brushed my hair. My skin prickled and I knew I wasn't alone. A dense cloud of mist floated up from the churning water. Aunt Teresa's face formed in the swirling mass of vapors. She was even more beautiful than I remembered. She smiled at me, and winked.

In that moment I felt the wire restraints that had bound my heart for so many years, severed. My soul filled with the warmth of a hundred summer suns and I wanted to laugh and cry all at the same time. I reached for her, to embrace her forgiveness—to tell her how sorry I was and how much she was missed.

My fingers touched only the rising mist from the churning waters. I drew the moisture to my lips and kissed each finger, sealing my farewell to Aunt Teresa. I knew without a doubt that I would see Aunt Teresa again someday.

THE GRAPE FIELDS
By
Mary Benton

Mama placed the lunch basket in the front seat of the old '38 Plymouth and slid in beside it. Daddy revved the engine, causing it to sputter in the early morning air.

As the youngest and only girl, I was sandwiched in the backseat between my two older brothers, Cyril and Dave. Picking buckets were wedged in between our legs.

The muggy stillness of late August closed around me. It was going to be a hot day in California's San Joaquin Valley.

We drove down the dirt drive of our small, rural home with our family dog, Ginger, trotting alongside. As soon as we reached the paved road, Ginger stopped, gave us a dejected look and turned back. I wished mightily I could've turned back with her.

Leaning across Cyril, I looked up at the mountains to the east. Orange-tinted light radiating from behind the Sierra cast Sawtooth Peak, and the miniature clusters of pines that dotted the distant ridges, in black silhouettes. How cool it would be under those pines, plus miles away from the hated grape fields that were our destination.

"I punched Cyril on the leg. "Do you see that deer under that tree?"

"What tree?" Cyril asked, frowning.

"The one on that far ridge. See, the sun is just hitting it."

68

Cyril's upper lip curled. "One of these days your lies are going to get you in a whole lot of trouble."

I grinned. In my imagination I could see the deer clearly.

The drive into the small town of Yettem didn't take long. Tellalian's grocery store dominated the small settlement. Its unpainted board-and-bat siding was toasted brown with age and splintered from years of exposure to the Valley's heat. Narrow windows on the second floor reflected the rays of the rising sun. A hitching rail to one side of the building spoke of bygone days.

"If you kids work hard picking grapes today, we'll stop on our way home and get a cold soda pop," Daddy promised. My mouth watered at the thought of a tingly Nehi strawberry soda.

Past the store, and the raisin-drying yards, six or seven faded clapboard houses lined the edge of the road. Constructed in the same design, their backyards bled into the dusty edges of a grape field.

Several miles beyond the small town, Daddy turned off the road and crossed a large canal. The bottom was dry, the sand sculpted in wave-like designs by the summer runoff. Dust rose in back of the car as Daddy continued down the silt-covered road. At last he pulled under a clump of cottonwoods and parked alongside several other cars and small trucks.

Daddy and Mama stepped out, we kids followed a little more slowly. Daddy adjusted his felt hat against the morning sun and Mama pushed a broad-brimmed straw hat over the red and white bandana she wore tied around her head. Neither of my brothers nor I had hats. I was lucky to have shoes. White shoes, several sizes to big and with torn stitching along the sides, courtesy of my cousin Eleanor's hand-me-downs. No socks. The sand that filled my shoes sifted out freely from the torn sides.

The man who owned the vineyard was talking to the workers as they arrived. Daddy informed him that we kids would be helping. The man grunted and gave Cyril and me a hard look. I sensed trouble.

"Make sure those kids don't get any sand into the trays."

"They know what they're doing," Daddy assured him.

Following Mama and Daddy into the field, I could already feel the dampness on my forehead.

A boy I knew from school was walking behind a group of grownups. He didn't look any happier than I was. His name was Melvin. He was quiet, wore torn and dirty clothes, and never looked directly at anyone.

Daddy selected two rows and tacked his cards on the end posts. He and Mama started cutting the seedless Thompson grapes from the vines and filling their buckets. My older brother, Dave, who was twelve, helped Mama on her row. Cyril and I picked up handfuls of the paper trays stacked at the end of the row. It would be my job to lay each sheet of the brown, waxed paper on the ground in the avenue between the grape rows and then spread the grapes on it that Cyril dumped. Sounded simple, but for a nine-year-old, being careful wasn't something my parents pointed to with pride.

Cyril was built like a red fire plug. It soon became a game to him. He would pile the grapes in a heap, then hurry back to get more so he could complain how slow I was.

As the morning wore on, Cyril became bored, and my determination to keep ahead of him, waned. Any enthusiasm I felt for the promised soda was lost in black pearls of sweat, burning feet, and blistered face and arms. I looked up to see the owner of the field coming up the avenue behind us. His image wavered in the heat waves that hovered close to the ground. When he drew even with Daddy, he spoke.

"Your kids are no good. They're getting sand into the trays."

My heart started beating faster. Would Daddy yell at us? It was my shoes' fault, I decided. It seemed they had a mind of their own. When I wanted to stop or turn, they just shuffled on.

Daddy walked over to us. I could see his face was set. No one called us kids "no good." He reserved that right for himself.

"Try to be a little more careful, Spud," he said to me. My name is Patricia, but Daddy always called me Spud.

"It's the shoes, Daddy," I said quietly. "I'll take them off."

"Well, see what you can do." He spoke more harshly to Cyril. I suppose since Cyril was ten, Daddy thought he should do better.

At first, working barefoot was fun. Before long though, I was hopping like a sand flea on hot bricks as I laid the trays down and straightened the grapes to an even depth. In my haste to seek relief in the shade of the vines for my scorched feet, I kicked even more sand onto the trays.

At last noon arrived and we walked back to the trees and our waiting lunch. When we reached the car, I saw Daddy talking to the owner. When Daddy came up to the car, he spoke to Mama.

"Mr. Yahnian said Cyril and Spud can't help anymore. They'll have to stay at the car for the rest of the day."

Mama rubbed her sweat-streaked face with a bandanna. "Dave can take over laying the trays. It will be okay."

Mama handed me a Spam and mustard sandwich. I bit into the fatty, boiled meat and wiggled my bare feet into the loamy soil, letting it sift through my toes. To sit in the shade of the trees for the rest of the day was all right by me.

When everyone returned to the field after lunch, I noticed that Melvin was also sidelined. He sat quietly on the running board of a rusty Dodge coupe, flipping through a dog-eared comic book. I stared at the colorful images of *Felix the Cat,* and wondered if Melvin would lend it to me when he finished.

For the next hour I drew pictures in the dirt with a stick while Cyril banged rusty nails into the end of a broken lug box with a rock. I found the other end of the smashed packing crate and attempted to join him in building a toy car. Lost in his own world, he ignored me.

I wandered back to the car and retrieved the tire pump. Pushing the handle down while pointing the hose at the ground, I carved miniature ditches in the loose soil. A line of large, black ants became the victims of girl-induced hurricanes, sending them skittering across the dirt. Frantic, the ants zigzagged around, searching for the column they were marching in. It wasn't long before this too, became tiresome. Having nothing to do but sit in the shade all day wasn't as much fun as I thought.

It occurred to me that Melvin might be finished with his comic book. I looked around, but didn't see him. I hadn't noticed him leaving, and wondered if he took the book with him.

Looking for something else to do, I remembered the canal bed. It would provide a fresh place to play. The canal curved along the edge of the grape field and it didn't take long for me to walk the short distance. The banks were covered in elderberry bushes and willows. I pushed my way through the brush and looked downward. I was startled to see an older man and a young boy standing in the bottom next to a willow bush. The boy was Melvin.

I crouched in the weeds. Melvin's britches were down around his ankles. His white bare boy parts contrasted sharply with the tan of his face. His arms hung limply at his sides. His face glistened with tears. The man laughed, said something I couldn't hear, and then placed his hand on Melvin's privates.

Placing both hands over my mouth, I scrunched lower. Had Melvin hurt himself? Was that man his father? I must have made a noise because the man whirled around and looked up. His face twisted in anger. He pushed Melvin away and turned to climb the steep bank toward me. Panic shot through me like I'd been stung by a wasp. I jumped and ran, not stopping until I reached the safety of the car.

"What's wrong?" Cyril asked. "Someone see you taking a whiz?"

For a moment I was tongue-tied. I didn't know how to tell Cyril what I had seen.

"There was a man in the bottom of the canal," I said, trying to catch my breath. "I think he was hurting Melvin. He saw me and started chasing me."

"I don't see anyone chasing you. How do you mean, hurting? Was he hitting him?"

"No. He was…you know, sorta touching Melvin's privates."

"Oh, you're so full of baloney."

"Go see for yourself," I asserted.

Cyril rose to his feet and dusted off his knees. He didn't seem in any particular hurry to check out my story. Picking up a thick piece of limb, he walked toward the canal bank. At school, Cyril would start a fistfight at the slightest insult. He was tough, and he wasn't afraid of anything.

"Make the man leave him alone," I hollered after him.

It seemed forever before I saw Cyril returning. I hunkered in the back seat of the car, clutching my knees to my chest.

Cyril peered in the window at me. "There wasn't anyone there. Are you sure you're not making this up?"

"Cross my heart and hope to die," I said, shaking my head and making crisscross signs over my chest. "I saw them."

"I think you're lying again." Cyril tossed the club aside and returned to his imaginary world of cars and trucks.

My heart was still hula dancing in my chest as I peered nervously at the cars and pickups parked around us. I didn't see anyone lurking about. The inside of the car was stifling with the smell of oil and gas. Sweat, dripping into my eyes, was making them sting. My legs felt weak as I crawled out of the car and sat on the fender. It was a little cooler there, but not much. Questions swirled in my head. Should I go to the vineyard and see if Melvin had returned to the field? Should I tell Daddy?

If I did tell, I'd probably get yelled at for wandering away from the car. It might be best not to set Daddy off. He was mad enough that Cyril and I messed up and caused the rest of the family to work harder.

I passed the rest of the afternoon using clods as baseballs. Tossing them in the air, I would swing at them with a stick, smashing them into powdery dust.

When it was quitting time, I was more than ready to go home. I glanced anxiously over to the car Melvin had been sitting on. I didn't see him, but a man and a lady were standing by the car, talking. I didn't recognize the man as the one I saw in the canal. The thought that a stranger was doing those things to Melvin made my shoulders crawl up around my neck.

I felt a poke in my ribs, and yelped.

"Get in the car," Dave growled. "I'm tired."

On the way home we sailed right on by Tellalian's. No stops for cold sodas. Daddy pushed his hat back and turned to Mama.

"We don't need to come back to this job. Without Cyril and Spud's help we can't make enough. I'll come back in the morning and collect our pay."

A deep guilt settled into the pit of my stomach. It was my fault that Daddy was going to quit. I felt sorry for Dave. He deserved a soda.

****

The next morning Daddy took off early to pick up the money for our previous day's work. He told Mama he would be back shortly and take her into town to buy groceries.

It was late afternoon before Daddy returned. Dave was sitting on the porch reading. Cyril and I were under the chinaberry tree, building a miniature town out of mud. When Daddy got out of the car, his hat was cocked at an angle. That meant most of the pay had already been spent on drink.

Silently, Dave stepped from the porch and headed for the barn. When Daddy drank, he and Mama quarreled.

I also decided to abandon the mud town and move to the other side of the house. Only Cyril stayed.

On the far side of the house I sat on the ground under the kitchen window. Ginger followed and flopped down next to me. It was cool there and I could hear Mama and Daddy talking.

Mama's voice had already risen.

"How much did you spend on liquor?"

"Not much. If you're ready, I'll take you to the store."

"I'm not going if I have to ask for credit. If you can't save enough money back to buy groceries, what good is it to have the children help?"

"Hell, woman, you should be grateful that I quit. That's why I had to have a drink. I couldn't stomach what happened out there."

"Why? What happened?"

"Some kid's missing. I guess the parents aren't worth killing, but they're yelling that someone kidnapped him."

I quit drawing my pictures in the dirt and stood, leaning close to the wall. My heart was clattering so loud I had to strain my ear drums to hear.

"When did he go missing?" Mama asked.

"Heck if I know. I think yesterday. They claim they left him up by the cars at noon and when they came in, he was gone. That sorry excuse of a sheriff asked if I knew anything about it. I didn't like his tone."

"Did you ask the kids if they saw anything?"

Panic sent a shiver down my spine.

"Naw. The only two that have any sense scattered like wild turkeys when I drove up."

"While I get ready, ask Spud if she saw a little boy up by the cars."

I slid down the wall, wishing I'd told Daddy about what I'd seen. I searched my options. I could lie and say I didn't see anything, or I could circle back around to the front of the house and hope Cyril ended up with half the blame.

I just made it back to the chinaberry tree when Daddy stumbled down the front stoop.

"Hey, you two," Daddy said, his voice serious. "Did either of you see a little boy up by the cars yesterday afternoon?"

Cyril frowned at me and then flung mud from his fingers as he shifted his attention to Daddy. "There was some kid Spud knew. I think his name was Melvin. Spud claimed she saw him down in the canal with some older guy who was messing with Melvin's privates. When I went to check it out, there wasn't anyone there. I think she made the whole thing up."

Daddy hitched his britches up and staggered a few steps closer to me. "You what?"

I chanced a quick look at him. His face was white. I was in big trouble.

Daddy whirled sharply toward the house. "Helen!" He took a step, then turned back and grabbed my arm.

"You're gonna tell your mama exactly what you saw and why you were at the canal in the first place."

I had to scramble to keep up with Daddy as he climbed the steps. Never saw Daddy sober up so fast.

Mama's face was creased in annoyance as she gathered her purse under her arm. "I'm ready," she said. "You don't have to yell."

Daddy shoved me toward Mama. "You listen to what your daughter has to tell you. I don't want to hear it. You can tell me later."

"I don't have a lot of time, Spud. Did you, or didn't you, see a little boy up by the cars yesterday?"

I nodded, thinking how I would tell Mama without getting myself into more trouble.

"I needed to go to the toilet," I began, and then related what I had seen and how the man started chasing me.

"Why on earth didn't you come to the field and tell us?"

"Because Cyril didn't believe me, so I figured you wouldn't either."

"But now a little boy is missing. For all we know, he could be dead!"

Melvin, dead...and it was my fault.

Mama clutched her purse to her bosom. "Your daddy and I have to go after groceries. You stay in the house until we get back."

"Are you going to tell someone about what I saw?"

"We have to. Are you sure the man wasn't someone you recognized from the field?"

I shook my head. "Not that I can remember."

"Do you think you can remember what he looked like?"

I screwed my eyes shut, seeing the man's face behind my eyelids. "Sorta," I said softly.

"It better be more than that." Mama's voice was strained. "If your daddy and I go to the sheriff with this, we don't want to look like fools. Worse yet, that our daughter is prone to making up stories."

After Mama and Daddy left, I went to the alcove that was once a large closet, but was now my bedroom. It was close and stuffy inside. A narrow cot was shoved against one wall. An orange crate wedged next to it held my underclothes. Nails in the wall provided a place to hang my dresses. I lay down on my bed and curled into a ball, clutching my china-head doll to my chest. Closing my eyes, I tried to bring up the image of the man so I could remember every detail. All I could see was Melvin's face, his tears, the helplessness. My guilt lay like bitter cider in my stomach.

****

It was close to sundown when Mama and Daddy came back. A police car was following them. My hands were clammy and I nearly suffocated myself from barely breathing.

The officer was huge, his khaki shirt straining against his wide shoulders. With the quietness of a barn cat, he entered the house and removed his hat. Mama offered him a chair, and after sitting, he took a notepad from his shirt pocket and settled it against one knee. The deep lines around his blue eyes crinkled as he smiled at me.

"I'm Deputy Raines, Patricia. I need to ask you a few questions."

I inched toward him and repeated my story, making sure I didn't add anything.

The officer's mouth twitched as he scribbled notes. "Can you describe the man to me, like how tall he was or if he was fat or skinny?"

"I don't know how tall he was 'cuz I was looking down at him. He seemed to have a round face and round eyes. That's all I remember."

The officer kept asking me questions and I kept wagging my head back and forth. I wasn't helping Melvin at all.

The deputy stood and smiled. "Thanks, Patricia. You've been a big help." He nodded at Mama, then turned and walked outside.

I let out a big sigh of relief. At least he didn't say it was my fault that Melvin was missing, maybe even dead.

We ate supper in silence. Daddy didn't want to hear anymore about it. Mama was also grim-jawed and only spoke to Dave. For some reason I felt ashamed, but couldn't figure out why. I wiggled my foot to and fro, my tongue itching to talk about Melvin and what might have happened to him.

****

The next morning Daddy, Mama, and Dave, left to go to another job. Cyril and I stayed home. Before they left, Mama instructed us that if we had a problem, we were to go to our nearest neighbors, the Poulsons, and ask for help.

After I finished with my chores, I went to my usual place to play, under the chinaberry tree in the front yard.

Cyril was still watering the garden when a green, frog-nosed pickup drove down the road in front of our house. Something about the truck looked familiar. I watched as it turned the corner and sped westward. I could still see the truck in the distance as it turned northward onto a dirt road that ran alongside an open field that lay behind our pasture. An abandoned house squatted crumbling among some eucalyptus trees in the middle of the field. It was my favorite place to explore when I had nothing else to do. The truck disappeared behind the trees.

I ran to the garden where Cyril was. "Do you remember a green pickup at the grape fields yesterday?" I asked.

Cyril threw a siphon pipe down and frowned. "Why?"

"I saw one going down the road. I think I remember seeing it."

"So? There're lots of green trucks around."

Disgusted with Cyril's response, I headed to the barn and climbed up on the hay bales. From my vantage point I could see across the vacant field and the old house in the distance.

Ginger hopped up next to me. She gazed at the open field and whined, giving me an anxious look. Did she know something, or did she just want to chase squirrels?

Before long, the truck drove out from behind the trees and continued down the road. Could the truck have anything to do with Melvin's disappearance?

I looked at Ginger. If Melvin was back there, Ginger could find him. I jumped from the hay stack. "Come on, Ginger. Let's go hunting."

I crawled through the sagging barbwire fence that separated our back pasture from the open field. It was dry, native land, filled with gray-skinned alkali spots, hog wallows, and riddled with squirrel holes. The image of the old abandoned house wavered in the heat. Large, brown grasshoppers clicked through the dry grass ahead of me as Ginger rambled through the weeds, her tail flagging her progress. Walking across the field, the oily smell of tar weed choked my nose and clumps of salt grass shattered and covered my legs in a fine, gray dust. Blue Jays screeched as I approached the house, and two buzzards lifted from their perches in the trees, sailing silently away.

The old house looked even scarier than I remembered and I hesitated, staring at the glassless windows and the surrounding ghost-like trees with their peeling trunks. The ground was covered ankle-deep in dried leaves and small limbs. I picked up a stick and started swatting at the debris, making sure there weren't any snakes or lizards lurking underneath.

A low growl from Ginger caught my attention. She stood frozen, the hair on her back standing up.

"What'cha got, girl?" I whispered.

Ginger stood facing the back porch, her small body crouched low. She took a step, her head darting back and forth.

I heard it then, a faint mewing sound. It sounded like a kitten was lost under the house. I bent down to look underneath. It was too murky to see anything. The sound came again and Ginger growled once more. I glanced at her and saw she was trembling. Rocking back on my heels, my mind did a little stutter. A cellar was located in that corner.

I patted my leg, encouraging Ginger to climb the steps with me. She hesitated a moment, then shot for home like a rifle bullet. Panic set in and I jumped from the porch and ran after her. Before clearing the trees, I stopped and turned back. I couldn't leave without looking in the cellar.

The door to the cellar was located in a small area just off the kitchen. I craned my neck into the open doorway. Leaves, swept in by the wind, lay in scattered heaps. Large holes gaped in the ceiling where rotting timbers dangled. A few pieces of broken furniture were still evident. I inched my way across the floor. A sound came from beneath me, almost a moan. My feet shuffled backward.

"Hello, anyone down there?" I called. My scalp prickled as a soft wind rustled through the old house, sending brittle leaves slithering across the floor.

Before my courage failed me, I moved to the trap door, and with both hands, yanked it open. I hopped back, half expecting a wild animal to come charging out. The only thing that came out was a sickly-sweet smell.

I edged closer and peered down into the darkness that shrouded the interior. I could barely see all the corners of the box-like space. A slight movement caught my eye.

In the dim light the outline of a small person took shape. Taking a deep breath, I made my way down the narrow ladder. My skin crawled at the thought of what I might discover. A gap in the ceiling boards allowed a sliver of light to fall on the prone figure and I immediately recognized Melvin.

He lay on his side, his face smeared with dirt, a torn and twisted tee-shirt wrapped around his upper body. His hands were clasped between boney knees, his shorts, a patch of whiteness in the sparse light. Leaning in closer, I saw that his hands and feet were bound with rope.

My stomach lurched and a bitter taste filled my mouth as I knelt and pulled at the ropes.

Melvin stirred and moaned.

"Wake up, Melvin," I said. "You've got to get out of here." My fingers fumbled at the knot. In desperation, I looked around for something to pry with. A movement at the top of the ladder caused my heart to lodge in my throat. A shadow loomed over the opening, and then a voice spoke.

"What do you think you're doing?" Cyril sounded annoyed. "And what is that smell?"

Relief washed over me. "It's Melvin," I gasped. "He's down here and he's messed all over himself. I think he's hurt real bad."

Cyril didn't question me. He clattered down the ladder, and walking over to Melvin, he gave a little shudder. "Criminey, he stinks."

"Can you get his hands untied?" I asked.

Cyril dug into his pocket and pulled out his jackknife. It didn't take long for him to have the ropes cut. "Help me get him to the ladder," he said. "I think I can carry him up."

I was scrambling to get hold of Melvin when something blocked the light coming from the cellar door. I glanced up.

A round face filled the opening. I let out a sharp screech, and the face disappeared. The door of the cellar slammed shut. Dust and grit rained down. Cyril and I stared at the ceiling as the sound of something heavy scraped across the floor. A thud against the cellar door made me cringe.

Cyril sprang into action. "No one's locking me in!" Arms and legs churned as he pulled himself up the ladder. He shoved his shoulder against the trap door, but it didn't budge. He jumped from the ladder, his eyes wild. Like an animal caught in a trap, I half expected him to start throwing himself against the walls.

"Your knife," I whispered. "There's a hole in the ceiling over in the corner. I think you might be able to chip away enough wood so we can get out."

Cyril nodded. "Yeah, that might work." Grabbing the ladder, he propped it against the wall next to the small opening and climbed up.

I hugged my elbows and glanced at Melvin. He hadn't moved. My fingers dug into my arms at the thought of what I might see if

I looked closer. I wanted out. Out to run away as far as possible. Walking in a small circle, I searched for other openings while Cyril jabbed at the heavy planks. That's when I spotted the missing adobe bricks at the top of one wall. They were hard to see because the darkened opening led to the space underneath the back porch.

"Dammit," Cyril swore. "I got a piece of wood in my eye." He hung his head, working one eyelid.

A snap and then a popping noise came from above. My hair fairly rose off my head as the smell of smoke drifted through the cracks in the ceiling. Cyril smelled it at the same time.

With one eye squeezed shut, and his other wild with terror, he yelled, "He's gonna burn us alive!"

There wasn't time to explain to Cyril about the bricks. "Get down," I said, shaking the ladder. I must've shaken it pretty hard, because Cyril lost his grip and fell to the ground.

Moving the ladder to the hole, I skimmed up the rungs. My hands dug into the soft dirt that was spilling from the opening. It would be a tight squeeze, but I was sure that both of us could fit through. I turned and looked for Cyril.

A layer of smoke hung next to the ceiling and I could barely make out Cyril's form dragging Melvin toward the ladder.

"What are you doing?" I choked, smoke stinging my eyes.

Cyril looked up at me, one eye still tightly closed. "We can't just leave him here. You crawl on through and I'll carry him up. Grab his arms and pull while I push."

I wasn't about to argue that Melvin was probably already dead and we were going to die too, if we didn't get out. I thrust my head through the opening, knocking out more bricks as I wiggled my way into the space under the porch. Red hot heat pressed against my back. I squirmed around to look down.

Cyril had already climbed the ladder, Melvin slumped over his shoulder.

Leaning into the cellar, I grabbed one of Melvin's arms and pulled, gaining leverage with my foot against the wall.

Cyril grunted. "Keep pulling."

Melvin was wedged in the opening. I crawled out from under the stoop, and turning, grabbed Melvin's limp hand. Digging my heels in, I tugged with all my might. The heat from the flames beat against my face and I was afraid to breathe. My vision blurred and my heart hammered in my chest.

Hands suddenly grabbed me around my shoulders, yanking me backward. "No," I screamed.

A voice spoke with authority. "Get back! We've got him."

Crouching on my hands and knees, I saw a man pick Melvin up and carry him away. I crawled toward the porch, looking for Cyril. Then I saw him. He was on his stomach, worming his way out from under the porch. I could barely see him as he stood and ran, flames flickering from his hair and shirt.

Strong arms curled around my waist, lifting me up. I started kicking.

"Stop it, little girl, I'm trying to help you."

We were clear of the smoke and heat when I realized the man carrying me was a policeman. He set me down and looked at me closely.

"Are you all right?"

My eyes stung and I couldn't see very well, but I nodded. I heard sirens blaring and squinted to make out a fire truck pulling up to the burning remains of the old house.

Our neighbor, Mrs. Poulson, walked up and placed an arm around my shoulders. "You best come with me, Patricia."

"What about Cyril? Where is he?"

"They've taken him and the little boy you both saved to the hospital."

I walked with Mrs. Poulson across the field to their house. "How did the police know to come?" I asked her.

"Your little dog, Ginger, came to our back porch, whining. My husband went out to have a look and saw the green truck parked on the old road and the smoke. He told me to call the police and the fire department."

"What about the round-faced man? Did the police catch him?"

"Yes, I believe they did."

***

I was all scrubbed and clean when Mama and Daddy picked me up. They'd been in to see Cyril at the hospital and told me he would have to stay for several more days, but he would be all right.

As soon as I was settled into the back seat, Mama took a deep breath. "Cyril told us what happened. He said you disappeared from the yard and he figured you went to explore the old house."

Mama turned around and glared at me. "Do you know how close you came to getting Cyril killed? If I wasn't so relieved that you're both alive, I'd give you a good whipping."

I ducked my head and pulled at the knots in my singed hair. "How is Melvin?"

Mama rubbed her forehead. "There were newspaper reporters all over that hospital. They're calling Cyril a hero for saving him. As far as I'm concerned, that boy's life wasn't worth almost losing the two of you."

The bit of news about Cyril being a hero caught in my craw. After all, I was the one who found Melvin.

"He's going to live though, isn't he?" I asked.

Mama's shoulders sank back against the seat. "Yes, they think so."

"And the man, who was he?"

"A so-called friend of the kid's family," Daddy put in. "I talked with Melvin's father at the hospital. He told me the man and his wife had been picking grapes a few rows over from them. Melvin's father said he hadn't actually noticed when the man left, or when he came back, because the fellow was prone to find an excuse to go somewhere, and leave his wife in the field working.

"The sick fool hid Melvin in that cellar to torture him. I think he intended to burn the house all along, figuring the kid's remains would never be found."

Daddy coughed out a dry laugh. "Imagine his surprise when he found you two idiots down in the cellar with Melvin."

My back stung where it had blistered from the heat and I leaned forward. "Why would the man want to hurt Melvin?"

Daddy was quiet a moment and I could tell he was searching for the right words.

"Spud, there are some men who like to hurt little boys … little girls too, for that matter. I can't understand why, anymore than you can. But these lunatics don't have any feelings of pity for the children they hurt, and they're not sorry for what pain they cause. Cruelty excites them. So they tell themselves that's what makes it all okay."

Mama whirled her head toward me. "And that's why, young lady, you need to mind when you're told to stay in the yard!"

I sank back against the seat. *How could anyone enjoy hurting someone like Melvin?* I thought of Cyril, lying in the hospital. Guilt pinched at my throat. In my mad scramble to escape, any thoughts of saving Melvin had flown out of my head. If it hadn't been for Cyril, Melvin, and perhaps even myself, would have been killed in the fire.

When we turned into our driveway, Ginger bounded out to greet us. Dave had all the lights on in the house and it looked warm and safe. The feelings of fear and sadness that I had been holding back, flooded through me. I stumbled from the car and pulled Ginger into my arms. Tears streamed down my face. Cyril and I had fussed ever since I could remember, and I had to admit, at times I did go out of my way to aggravate him. But at that moment, I was proud of my brother. He deserved to be treated like a hero, because he was.

Art Theft

She sits front row in drawing class. Mary's vain
of her tattoo. Its color and intricacy
impresses but it gives little
competition
to the grandeur of the darkly
twisted braid that teases my eyes.
My envious pencil makes her beauty my own.

2011 Sylvia Ross

Oak Trees

While poets talked, oak trees grew
Between their feet, grew strong branches
To hold up skies, grew strong roots
To crack roads, grew shiny leaves
To drift into those cracks.
While poets talked, oak trees grew
Beneath their feet, made mats of twigs
To house small spiders, opened up spaces
For pairing birds, grew rich acorns
To feed hungry ghost people.
While poets talked, grasses sprouted.
Lichens spread across granite outcrops.
Generations of herd animals grazed
And seedlings grew into forests
while poets talked.

2010 Sylvia Ross

-for the poets: Salinas, Mezey, Ginsberg, Dofflemyer, and Hernandez
Dry Crik Journal, John Dofflemyer, ed.,
Vol. VI, 2010, an online publication featuring
the work of contemporary western writers:
 www.drycrikjournal.org

Sylvia Ross

The Seagulls' Banquet

fragments of shell whitening on the beach,
traces of the fragging of one organism
by another

beauty emerges from destruction
a dawn walk's reminder that
living things survive only by interference
with the survival of other living things

so, looking for small kindnesses,
soft voices, a repudiation
of harsh and unwanted knowledge

I welcome denial that I am both abalone
and hungry gull, and hold back witness
that a broken shell is no more
beautiful than a beach sand feather.

1995 Sylvia Ross

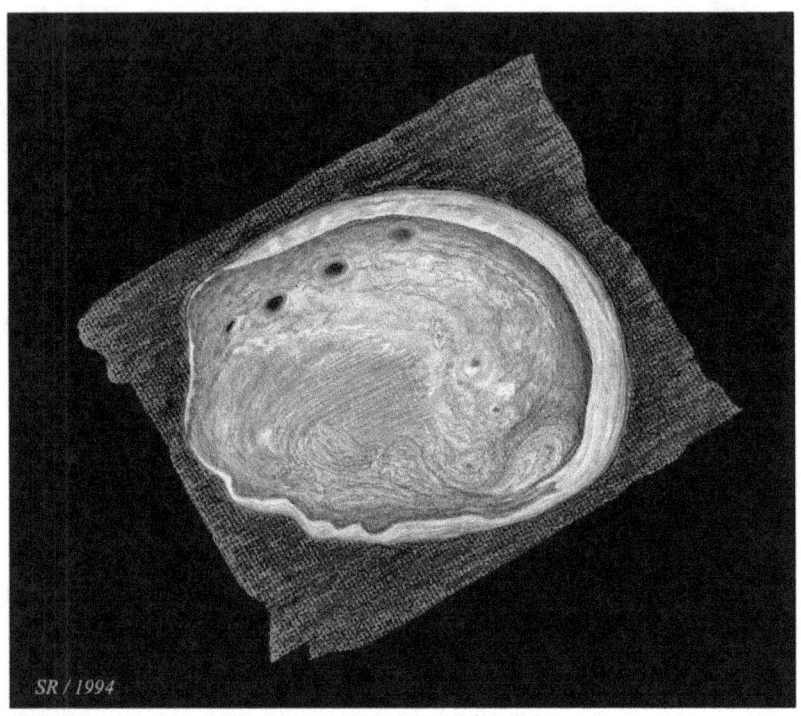

Ted's abalone shell prismacolor drawing, an exercise in photo-realistic rendering

Sylvia Ross   1994   (source ideation for The Seagulls' Banquet)

Love Dance

Desperate now and clever
with the slyness
of other mute women
like chained dogs, hobbled beasts,
I twist my head and writhing
try to break free.
Pulling back, recklessly then
I surge forward,
but he holds me tethered
by soft mouth, pale eyes.

I am as tightly collared
on the leash of his displeasure
as he is chained to the
taunting lead of mine.
These tortured movements
Give violent celebration
To each's own cruel option.

2003 Sylvia Ross

Program publication:
California Artists & Writers
ASAIL – MLA INT. CONFERENCE
San Diego, CA, December 2003

Sylvia Ross

Cultural Capitulation

Below the cold white sun and swooping crows,
skaggy branches reach for my old red truck.
I like the truck's bright color. Maybe the trees do too.
The grey trees long ago pushed past fence lines.
Brooms of eucalyptus branches scrape the windows.
Leaves block any view of the easement road.
I drive on and don't see a snake,
but the truck's wheels bump twice over its length.
In the mirror the banded snake lies in the ruts, dead,
only fit for crows. I stop the truck.
It's time to evict those damned foreign trees.
I can't worry whose property they're on. Not mine.
Oak belongs here. Eucalyptus doesn't.
I have saw and shears and axe, could strip this foreign
arboretum to the ground, take revenge on its trees
for the accidental killing of a snake.
The intrepid crows, longer residents
of this valley than any of my own indigenous ancients,
wheel in the air. They squawk and scold at my intent.
Crows live in these dubious trees, nest, adapt.
It's time to go home, to the sofa, to a cup of imported coffee,
to a consideration of snakes, Australian trees,
and the essential dominance
of crows.

Sylvia Ross   2011

Roundelay for Ghost Singers

 In the night most part of winter
When the fog drips wet and cold
Shadows weave beyond the fire
Sweet smoke calls forth old voices
Children hear ancient stories

When the fog drips wet and cold
Shadows weave beyond the fire
Sweet smoke calls forth old voices
Children hear ancient stories
In the night most part of winter

Shadows weave beyond the fire
Sweet smoke calls forth old voices
Children hear ancient stories
In the night most part of winter
When the fog drips wet and cold

Sweet smoke calls forth old voices
Children hear ancient stories
In the night most part of winter
When the fog drips wet and cold
Shadows weave beyond the fire

2007 Sylvia Ross

Vertebral Doggerel

Would it be so difficult to cope
with being an ant?
It might be nice to be
an ant or roach or scorpion,
often social, ever industrious.
One might hope
thoughts more relevant
would arise from neurons safely
inside an exoskeleton,
that ideas grand and illustrious
would find firing there superior-
to traveling a bony interior.

grass sr/2005

Grandpa's beard

Admonition

Don't give up touch, grandchildren.
feel beards, beads, fabrics, fibers, hair, reeds,
skin, yarns, piano keys, strings, rich planting soil, smooth stone.
Take delight in whatever intrigues your fingers.
e.e. cummings was right, and
"...feeling is first..."
2011 Sylvia Ross

MADERA COUNTY
By Sylvia Ross

Ernie squinted up his good eye and looked off across the fields. Over on Dominic's land beyond the road, black waves of old burn cut into the barley stubble. The burn ended in a long ditch that separated Dominic's property from the Miller ranch. Fence posts ran jagged along the edge of the far side of the road and long ruts crisscrossed where tires had dug into the dust during the summer. The fire didn't cross the road. On Ernie's land the wild barley had bleached over the summer. It still stood stiff and tall, waiting for Mueller's cows to chew it down. Ernie's other eye saw nothing.

He could scare children with his other eye. Of an afternoon or evening when she and Morris were in from fieldwork, he'd go down to Gussie's and sit out on her porch with Morris and scatter all those damn kids that hung around there. He thought about the kids, how they'd run and hide in the grapevines whenever they saw his rackety car pull up in front of Gussie's place. That old black woman got so mad at him. Sometimes he turned quickly when he was going onto her porch to make a face at the kids. He'd put his evil eye on them. Always made him chuckle, but Gussie'd get fluttery mad. Wanted him to get a patch for his eye. What'd he want to go and do that for? It'd get all sweaty and uncomfortable. He laughed to himself, thinking of Morris and Gussie. They were good friends, though he was about the only white man who came around to sit on their porch.

Over by the pump a child played, and from the chicken house's shade, the long tail of a dog poked out into the sunshine. The child was piling up dirt into mounds around the bucket that sat beneath the pump. She filled her hands with dirt and slowly let it seep out between her fingers.

La Vina District, Madera County ~ Ernest Bolden Cox and granddaughter

Ernie settled down in the swing and lit his pipe. He watched her play. Wasn't much like her mother. Ellen wouldn't like it, but he let the child run around in her underpants until the mosquitoes came out. Nobody was around his place to care what she wore on a hot day. Three-year-old kid didn't need pinafores or shoes. He sat in his swing, tasted the tobacco and watched her hug up the dirt and then let it down on the mounds. She straightened up and let the last of what she had in her hands filter out into the green water of the drip bucket.

"Child, you come and get out of that water," the old man called to her. He rocked slowly back and forth.

"I'm not in the water," she answered.

"I know you're not, but Boy and all them kittens drink out of there. Boy don't want to drink dirty water. How'd you like it if I gave you dirty water to drink?"

He heard her mumble something and he said, "You got something to say you better say it out clear."

She looked slanty at him and then yelled, "I'm where I'm aposed to be. You leave me alone."

The swing stood under a row of eucalyptus trees that grew on the east side of the yard. Between them and the house was an open area where Ernie left the car when he wasn't going anywhere. A hundred feet behind the house were some outbuildings, a chicken house and a two-seater outhouse. Closer to the house and a bit to the west was a windmill. Between the windmill and the kitchen door stood the pump. He had marked off the area for her. She was free as long as she stayed in the dusty triangle of the house and trees and outbuildings.

"Now you just behave yourself, or I'll put you over in the chicken yard and the chickens will peck your feet good."

She turned her back on him and didn't sass him anymore. He leaned his head back and was glad he had trees to put his swing under. Gussie and Morris didn't have one tree around that old shack of theirs. It just jutted out of the vineyard with no shade. 'Course the Italians always had plenty shade around them. Soon he'd get himself some pomegranates from Lidio and Mary Lou. Always get pomegranates from the Italians.

The girl got up and walked over to the swing. The old man watched her come up near him. She reached out her hand and rubbed it across the green and orange stripes of the cushions. She took both hands and began pushing the cushions until the swing was rocking. After a long time she said, "Grandpa, when's my mommy coming back?"

The old man took his pipe out of his mouth and spat onto the dirt by his feet. Then he reached out and tried to pull her up into the swing beside him, but she backed away. "Your mommy's got to tend to her business. She'll be back soon's she can."

"She promised."

"Your mommy lived here when she was a little girl like you."

He remembered all the years. It was just like now. Electricity was in past the Miller place now. He could have hooked into it but there was no need. "She played under these trees. When she got big enough she went down the road to La Vina School."

He closed his good eye and said, "Little girl, your grandma planted these trees nearly thirty years ago in 1911. They weren't so big then."

"Don't talk to me," she whispered.

But he kept on talking until she ran away from the swing. She ran past the car and past the stump where he killed chickens, past the long row of trees. She ran down the dusty drive toward the road. The old man watched her go, and then he got up and followed. She dropped down into the ditch that separated his forty acres from the road. He stood on the culvert crossing at the edge of the ditch and looked down at her. Sunlight filled up half the ditch and glinted the quartz sand that marked where the water had been last time it ran. Now the weeds growing down the sides of the ditch were old and prickly. The child slid to the bottom of the ditch and put her hands into the warm sand.

"Rattlesnakes will get you down in that ditch." Ernie stood and looked down at her and he was smiling. "You climb on out of there." His voice was soft and slow. He pronounced that last word, they-ya.

"No."

"Come on."

"No." She wouldn't look at him.

"Come on you get out of there. If you're a good girl, I'll take you hunting with me."

"When?"

"Tonight."

"You promise?"

"Yep."

She climbed up the side of the ditch, and they walked back to the house and went inside. He took a pot of cold coffee from the top of the woodstove and poured some out into a mug and used the hand pump at the sink to draw a glass of water for her.

"I want coffee too," she said.

Ernie nodded at her and poured a swish of dark liquid into her glass. The coffee swirled down making a pale amber spiral in the water. He put the pot back on the top of the stove and sat down beside her at the kitchen table. He pushed a small plate of leftover biscuits across the linoleum strip covering the table. She picked one up and dunked it in the glass. Ernie reached to the shelf above the table and got down a deck of cards. The old man laid out solitaire. She watched him for a little while, smugly drank her coffee, and then went outside to call the dog and share what was left of a second biscuit.

The old man went outside. It was mid-afternoon. The heat was glaring off the buildings and making their unpainted sides smell sweetish and rotting. The place was his and he took pleasure that it was aging along with him. He didn't plant anything. Things grew, cottontails, wild barley, field mice and horny toads, touch-me-nots and yellow poppies in season. But on his place the things that grew did it of themselves. Ernie didn't plow the soil. Gussie tried to talk him into planting the forty acres to cotton to make a profit, but he was independent. He didn't need to do that. Surgeons in Jacksonville during the Spanish-American War had given him a blind eye and a lifetime of headaches while treating him for brain fever. It bought him an army pension. The check every month paid for his beans, coffee and taxes. He could look out across his land and know it was his.

Boy whined and thumped his tail against the rough boards of the chicken house. Ernie scanned slowly past the windmill and saw a shape coming diagonally across the fields toward the house. The old man kept watching. The child saw him and went back into the house. Pretty soon Ernie could make out the checkered shirt and the rifle swinging and waved to Dos, and then he went to sit in the swing out of the sun. Dos' right arm stopped at the elbow and his sleeve was pinned up. But he could shoot pretty well. Better'n anyone would have thought.

The ground beneath the swing was littered with small dry eucalyptus horns. The day before the girl had made little pyramids of the small hard bits of debris from the trees. They formed an irregular circle of mounds around the base of one of the trees. As Dos slid his gun under the barbed wire, and spread the wire to step through, Boy came out and loped over to the swing where Ernie sat. The dog went slowly around the swing, circled and lay down, resting his head on one of the eucalyptus mounds.

Frank Doster crossed the yard. He bent down and put his gun on the ground again, and then squatted down beside it. He managed to take a pack of cigarettes from his shirt pocket and light up with one hand without losing his balance.

"Lidio got hisself in jail again." Doster was a young man, but he cackled out the words like an old crone or the squabbling poultry.

The old man looked at him but didn't answer.

"You got any money?" Dos asked.

The old man shook his head no.

"Goddam, Ernie. We got to get him out."

The old man took his time answering. "Why?" he said. "We didn't put him in."

"Well, shit, Ernie. We only need thirty bucks more an' we can get him out." Dos picked up some of the dry eucalyptus horns and tossed them under the canvas fringe of the swing to wake the dog.

The old man frowned at Doster's raw language, but it was a free country. "What's he done this time?"

"That damn Lee-dee-o got in a fight with Mary Lou down't the Italian store and Gina called the deputy. Can you beat that? She's Lee's cousin, and she called the law on him. Jackson was just outside gassing up and she went and hollered him into the store." Dos grinned and rubbed his jaw, "Jackson cuffed him and got him on drunk and disorderly. Damn fool of a Lee got no sense. Mary Lou aggravates him and he rises to her bait. Now she says they can just keep him. She don't care. Gina swore out the complaint because Lee knocked over a four-shelf display of Acme. Broke every bottle. Hell, Ernie, dove season'll be here and gone unless we get him out."

Ernie started to answer, but the screen door on the kitchen banged and interrupted his thinking. No one came out. He looked

up toward the house and the screen door banged again, and then
again.

"What you got in your house?"

"Little girl's here."

"I remember. You tole me she'd be here for a couple weeks.
Why'd your daughter bring the kid up here? She so busy down
L.A. she can't take care of her own kid?"

"She was married over in Yuma this week past. They need time
to get settled down."

"Who's she marrying this time?" Dos reached over and pulled
his rifle and moved it closer to him. The kid might come out of the
house, think it was a toy.

"That Hungarian, Joe. You remember. She brought him up here
last spring. They stayed a couple of days. Fished. Took some
salmon out of the San Joaquin."

"Marryin' that old furr-i-ner?" Dos looked surprised and then
smiled. "Hell, Ernie, that girl of yours coulda stayed round here
and married a Mex. She didn't need to go down to L.A to find
som'un couldn't speak English right. He's near as old as you."

Ernie just looked off across the yard and fields for a while and
then he said, "He's a good man. He's done all right for himself.
She's better off with him than a ragged five acre Okie."

"You're sumthin' better, old man?"

"I'm not a ragtag one-armed dustbowl Okie."

The two men laughed together for a time and then the screen
door began banging again. The old man stood up and took a big
handkerchief out of the pocket of his overalls. He wiped the
moisture that had collected around his blind eye and put the
handkerchief back into his pocket.

Dos got up too, slower, and moving almost sullenly. He began
walking across the yard. "Be back by tomorrow morning, for it

gets too hot. See if you can figger out how we can get Lee out. Only need thirty dollars, Ernie." He stopped for a moment and added, "We gonna need your car too. Morris says he needs a new clutch afore his truck'll go anywhere. We get the money, you can driver us to town to bail Lee out."

Ernie nodded. "See what I can do." Lee was always ready to lend a hand. Mechanical. Couldn't have replaced the shaft on the windmill last winter without Lee. He owed him thirty dollars. The old man gave a gesture with his hand and a little tuck of his head to let Dos know he was in agreement.

Doster started off across the fields. The girl in the house was lying on the cool linoleum, using her feet on the door.

Ernie didn't clean her up for supper until the sun was low. He helped her wash, get her blouse and overalls on, and buckled her sandals. It was too hot to cook, so they ate cold canned beans and thick slices of salami with muscat grapes. He didn't make fresh coffee. He poured cold bitter liquid left from the noon meal into his mug and put some for her in a china cup he'd half filled with canned milk. He added a little water and let her stir a spoon of sugar in the mix. After they ate, he rinsed the dishes off by the pump at the sink. The girl went back outside and ran to the swing. Through the screen he watched her jump up into it and rock back and forth while he cleaned up. Boy curled beneath her. She reached down to pet him and fell out.

It was getting dim in the kitchen. Ernie reached up behind the stovepipe and pulled out a little tin box. Inside there were five ten-dollar bills. He put three of them in his wallet and then put the two remaining bills back into the box and stuck it back into its place. The old man counted out the money in his wallet and it came to thirty-one dollars and sixty-seven cents. He put the wallet back into the pocket of his overalls, lit the kerosene lamp and put it on the table. The kerosene's smell drove out the night smells of wild barley and eucalyptus that were coming through the screen door. He decided to get makings for corn bread set out for the next morning.

The girl came running to the door. She stood there watching him from the other side of the screen. The lamplight was bright in her eyes and the old man smiled at her but she didn't smile back.

"Better come in, now, honeybee," he said.

"You promised. It's night now."

He winked his good eye at her and said, "You go up by the car. I'll be 'long pretty soon. Got do my chores yet."

Ernie watched her run to the car. She couldn't open the door, so she sat on the running board. He finished in the kitchen. This was the time of day he liked best. The sun was all gone but for the greenish streak just above the Coast Range, and the chickens were settling down. If he remembered to listen each night, just about now a cool west breeze would come up rustling through the eucalyptus to temper the day's heat.

He hooked the wire door to the chicken yard against coyotes and drew the calf to the barn with some of the chicken grain. He dropped the latch beam securely. Then went back to the house. He counted the eggs in the bowl on the shelf above the table. There were nineteen. Tomorrow he'd stop by Gina's and he'd trade eggs for produce. He turned down the lamp and went outside. A couple of gunnysacks lay in a pile by the back steps and he reached down and picked one up. Throwing it over his arm, he started for the car.

The girl said, "You forgot your gun."

"I don't need a gun, honey."

"You made me wait too long and big ol' giant mosquitoes came and bit me."

He turned toward her and said, "Let me see." But she pulled away from him.

"What are we going to hunt?"

The old man pushed in the clutch and threw the car into reverse. The little girl fell against him as the car jerked back down the long dirt drive toward the road. As the car bumped across the wooden boards over the ditch culvert, she straightened up enough to see out the windows and said, "You forgot to turn on the lights."

He snapped on the switch and one lone headlight shone out from the old ford toward the house. The car backed onto the road. He straightened out the wheel and headed south toward the river. The last green streak of sky had gone black.

"What are we going to hunt?" she asked again, and her voice was impatient.

The old man looked down at her and said, "We going to get some food for Boy 'cause he's an old dog and can't get it for himself." Then he pushed down on the accelerator until the car hit thirty. They were going fast. Crickets were chirping in the night in black ditches on either side of the road. They went faster. For a few miles they saw no other cars and the lights in ranch houses came in view and disappeared quickly. Then in the darkness Ernie could smell riverweeds over the smell of alfalfa. Ernie began to sing a song he taught her called *Standing on the Promises*. The car was going so fast it was shivering. Bugs smashed themselves against the window of the car. Way off ahead of them something flashed across the road. Then, just behind it a rabbit froze, blinded by the one white light of the old rackety car. The old man swerved the car and the car raced toward the animal. There was a thud. Ernie hit the brake and the car skidded to a stop. Ernie cranked the car into reverse and backed up. He turned off the engine and put his pipe up on the dashboard. He reached down on the floor of the passenger side, grabbed up the gunnysack, and got out. The girl watched him from through the open door of the car, then knelt high enough on the seat to watch through the windshield.

Ernie walked forward into the white light of the headlight. He bent down and picked up the quivering rabbit by its hind feet and it hung still. Pink coils slipped down from its belly. With his free hand he worked the mouth of the sack open and dropped the dead animal into it. Then he wiped his hands on the kerchief that hung from his overalls pocket. He came back to the car and dropped the sack down on the floor below her. She pulled her feet up on the seat. They went on. He kept on singing the old hymns he'd taught her, *Rock of Ages*, *Peace in the Valley*, *Take My Hand, Precious Lord*. They got two more rabbits that night.

The night closed in all around them. They drove home slowly. She wiggled closer to her grandfather, and he put his arm around her. He was a one eyed man with in a one eyed Ford, and he could drive one armed just fine. He began singing, *"Bye baby bunting, Grandpa's gone a-hunting, to fetch a little rabbit skin, to wrap his baby bunting in."*

"I'm not a baby."

"Tomorrow we'll go to town for ice cream."

"You promise?"

"Yep. First, we'll go to the courthouse."

"What's a cordhouse?"

(1968, pub.1969, *BACKWASH*, Vol. 7, No.2, Fresno State College Association, Omar Salinas, ed., revised as memoir 2010.

BROKEN FARMER
By Donna Leach

He snapped a long, thin branch from the peach tree growing in his front yard. After removing the leaves, he tested the flexibility by swishing it through the air in fast diagonal movements. "It's a good switch," the farmer grunted, satisfied with the selection. He knew a good switch from a bad one after the many beatings he received while growing up. However, he'd dished out his fair share of whippings through the years as well.

"See this?" he yelled and held up the thin branch. "I'm gonna whip the tar out of you." He scanned the field beside his weathered farmhouse. They were hiding out there somewhere.

The old farmer stumbled to the edge of the cornfield holding the switch in one hand and a whiskey bottle in the other. "I'm gonna get you, you little sons-of..." his voice trailed off as he chugged down the last of the liquor. He wiped droplets from the stubble on his chin with the back of his hand and tossed the empty bottle into the field.

A woman appeared on the front porch drying her hands on the apron she wore. "Pa," she shouted. "Time to come in for supper."

He ignored her and crossed the yard to the melon patch on the west side. "You think you're pretty clever, don't ya? You didn't think I'd see ya, but I did."

"Everett, supper's ready," she repeated.

He turned and glanced at the porch, seeing the silhouette of his wife with her arms folded against her waist like he'd seen her do a hundred times before.

"Come on now before your food gets cold," she called.

The old man swiped his hand through the air. "Can't you see I'm busy?"

"I see an old fool stumbling around shouting at an empty field."

Everett rocked back on his heels and cocked his head. "There, did you hear that?"

A breeze rustled the leaves of the tree. "All I hear is the wind. You come inside now and stop this foolishness."

"Ah, you go on and leave me be. You ain't good for nothing no-how."

The woman threw her hands up, shook her head, and went inside.

Everett cocked his head again, listening to the faint voices blowing on the breeze. "I hear ya laughing. You think it's funny, don't ya? You won't be laughing much longer."

He rounded the backside of the house and headed for the barn. Leaning his ear against the barn door, he whispered. "I know what you're up to. You're waiting for it to get dark. You think I won't catch ya then."

Everett swung the door open with a sudden jerk. Chickens clucked in protest at the intrusion. "Ya'll come on out now. I ain't funnin' with ya." He stepped inside the dimly lit barn. "Spare the rod, spoil the child. That's what the good book reads. Like my pappy always said, can't have any spoiled children. We got to whip the old devil right out of your hide."

After searching the barn, the farmer came out into the yard. He rotated in a circle shouting in all directions. "All right, I done gave you a chance to come out peacefully, but ya'll are starting to grate on me now. I'm gonna give ya to the count of five to get off my land 'cause I'm about to get my shotgun." Everett hiccupped off a five count as the last of the sun disappeared in the west.

He stomped through the back porch to the kitchen. A trail of dried mud clods followed his path.

"Well, it's about time," the woman said while rinsing a bowl at the sink. "I was ready to give your supper to the hogs."

"Might as well, it tastes like hog slop anyhow." He flopped onto the chair at the table, his plate of food in front of him.

"Everett, why do you talk to me that way?"

"What way?" he asked, while spooning mashed potatoes into his mouth.

"Hateful like." She brushed a lock of hair from her forehead. "You treat me worse than a stray dog."

He grunted and looked up at her. "Ah, I was just funnin' with ya."

"Well, I've had as much funnin' from you as I can stand. I'm leaving." She untied the apron and tossed it on the counter.

"Where ya going?"

"I'm going back home to see my family." She marched through the living room, glancing back at him as she scooped up a set of car keys from a side table. "Everett, something is broken inside you." The door slammed behind her.

"Wait," he shouted. "Clara?" He choked on his food and broke into a hard cough, spewing clumps of potatoes across the kitchen floor.

Everett pushed away from the table and staggered into the living room. He removed his shotgun from the rack over the fireplace, shoved some shells in his pocket, and sat in his recliner with the rifle across his lap. "I'm ready for ya," he shouted. "Come on back, you little thieves. See what you get." He reclined the chair and closed his eyes, mumbling softly. "Who needs her anyway, she ain't good for nothing no-how."

At a quarter past eleven, a dog howling in the distance woke Everett from his drunken slumber. "Huh, Clara?" he mumbled. His legs were stiff from sleeping in the recliner and he had trouble standing. "Clara," he shouted. "Come help me out of this damn chair." When she didn't come to his aid, he scooted to the edge of the seat and used the shotgun as a cane to draw himself up to his feet. "Clara," he called again. "Where are you?" He shuffled from room to room, but couldn't find his wife.

A dull thump sounded outside. Everett raised the barrel of his shotgun and staggered to the front door. He stepped onto the porch. "Who's out there?" His voice cut through the stillness of the night. "You better get on out of here before I spray buck-shot all over ya." Not even a cricket chirped.

"Clara, is it you?" Everett stepped off the porch into the light of a full moon. "I've been looking for you. Why don't you answer?"

Another thumping noise came from behind him, and he spun around toward the peach tree. Several peaches lay on the ground. "Well, why did ya go and do something like that?" He ran to the edge of the cornfield and yelled. "Them are my peaches, my corn and my melons, you sons-of-bitches. I'm gonna get you." He raised the gun and took aim, blasting through the corn stalks. "How ya like that?"

The old farmer crossed the yard to the melon patch and blasted another round through the field. "Run and hide, I'll find ya. I'll find all of ya, if it takes all night."

Everett circled around the house. He dropped down on one knee, fumbling with the shells, trying to reload his gun, losing most of his ammunition on the ground. He stood and randomly fired into the field, hoping to get lucky and hit one of the little thieves. Everett listened as a breeze rustled through the corn stalks. "I hear ya. You ain't gonna get away this time."

He walked into a row of the cornfield. A shadowy figure stood a few yards ahead of him. He raised the barrel of his shotgun and blasted a round. "Yahoo," he cheered as a hat blew into the air. Everett ran toward his victim. The old scarecrow was now minus a head. He made a fist and shook it. "I guess ya'll think that's pretty funny, don't ya?"

A set of headlights appeared in the distance and turned down the farmer's long dirt road. Everett walked out of the field and climbed onto his porch. He aimed his shotgun toward the approaching car. It stopped before reaching the house. A door opened and someone stepped out.

"Who are ya?" Everett shouted.

"Everett, don't shoot. It's Sheriff Barsley."

"What do you want?"

"Lay the gun down. I want to talk to you."

Everett lowered the barrel. "Sheriff Barsley?"

"Yes, get rid of that shotgun so we can talk."

Everett stumbled forward. "Well, those little hoodlums are robbing me blind. I got to protect my harvest."

The sheriff came out of the darkness holding a flashlight with one hand and the other resting on his holstered pistol. "Please, lay the gun on the ground, Everett."

He looked at his gun and then at the sheriff. "Why?"

"I don't want you to accidentally shoot me."

Everett laid the shotgun on the porch step. "All right, it's on the ground. Now help me catch those melon thieves."

Sheriff Barsley walked briskly toward him and picked up the weapon. "What's going on out here? Your neighbors called in saying they heard gunshots from your farm."

"It's that boy and his friends. They've been stealing my melons and my corn. Look what they did to my peaches."

"What boy?"

"Clara's boy. Chad and his friends are the ones doing it."

"Everett, have you been drinking tonight?"

"Well, I had a couple earlier, but that don't change nothing. Those boys need to be taught a lesson. They need a good lickin' with a switch broken across their backside."

"Everett, how old are those boys?"

"I don't know, old enough to know better, at least twelve or thirteen."

"Chad is forty years old," Sheriff Barsley said.

"Naw," Everett mumbled. He rubbed the back of his neck. "I saw them boys out in my field stealing my melons."

"You don't farm anymore, Everett. You retired years ago. These fields are leased out, remember? Chad farms this land with his boys. That's who you saw in the fields."

A crease formed in the old man's forehead. "Yeah? Yeah, I retired. I don't farm no more." Everett stumbled off the porch. "I can't find Clara anywhere."

"Clara died ten years ago," Sheriff Barsley said.

"No," Everett gasped, shaking his head in disbelief. "It can't be."

"I'm afraid so. Clara died in an automobile accident on her way to visit her kin. You really shouldn't drink, Everett. It confuses you. Let's go inside and get you into bed. You'll feel better in the morning."

"Yeah, yeah … tomorrow will be better."

The Sheriff guided Everett to his bed and settled him in after pulling his boots off. "I don't want to hear about you shaking sticks at Chad's boys while they're working the land anymore. And you better not take any potshots at anyone. You hear me? Chad's going to commit you to a mental hospital if you keep carrying on like this. He's a hard working farmer and a good stepson to you. His wife brings supper over for ya every evening. They're the only family you got. Now get some sleep. Good night."

"Good night, Sheriff," Everett sighed.

As the old man rolled to his side, a tear trickled down his leathered cheek. "I'm sorry, Clara. You were right. I think something is broken inside me."

He felt soft fingers brushing the side of his face, wiping the tear away. A whispering voice soothed him. "Now, don't you fret none. Everything will be just fine."

Everett smiled and closed his eyes. "Goodnight Clara. See ya in the morning."

From the pillow next to him, the farmer heard his wife's tender voice, "Goodnight, Everett."

WORN AND TORN
By Donna Leach

We were loaded and carted away from the only home we ever knew. "Where are they taking us?" I asked Marty.

"They're getting rid of us. That's the only reason they're taking us off the plantation," he answered.

When we reached the sales yard, Marty told me not to speak to anyone. Poor Marty, he didn't realize a worse fate awaited us if we kept silent. He should have listened to me.

"Just keep your mouth shut," he said.

"But, they want us to talk, it entertains them," I tried to tell him.

"You talk too much," was all he said.

My dress was torn, dirt stained my bare feet, and my once silky hair hung in a tangled mess. Marty said it was good to look worn and torn. If nobody bought us the master would have to take us back to the plantation.

We were slaves, subject to the whims of those holding us, existing for their amusement. Our shabby appearance was evidence of the neglect we suffered at their hands. Our master sent us to the auction block along with unwanted household goods including the piano that the master's daughter once played.

They placed Marty and me with the other rejects. Potential buyers poked and prodded at us. I tried to hide behind the others who were dressed in rags, some were naked and scarred.

Marty wouldn't cower in the back row with me; he stood prominently on the platform and stubbornly refused to speak no matter how much they tried to force him. One man shook him with such velocity that I thought his eyeballs were going to fall out of his head. He didn't crack. Even though he suffered relentless poundings, he never uttered a word. Finally, they knocked his battered body to the ground and stomped on him as they walked off.

No one helped Marty. I wanted to go to him, but I was afraid. He lay on the cold ground alone and unable to move.

The piano rumbled down the ramp, pushed by its new owner. Watch out, I wanted to shout when I saw it headed for Marty, but it was too late. The piano flipped over on top of him, smashing Marty with a horrid cracking sound. My poor friend. What was wrong with these people? Did they have no compassion, no mercy? They were more concerned about the piano than Marty.

As I stood filled with sadness and despair, I made a decision. I wouldn't talk either. No matter the consequences, I would not give them the satisfaction.

One by one, the other pitiful outcasts were sold until I stood all alone. My turn finally arrived. A woman approached holding the hand of a small girl. The little girl wore a pretty pink dress; ribbons flowed from her long locks, the same type of ribbons I once wore in my hair. I closed my eyes and hoped for a swift end. To my surprise, I felt a soft hand brush across my cheek.

"Ah, poor thing," a gentle voice whispered.

Then, I was carefully turned and inspected. A strange pulling sensation tugged on my back. My mouth opened. I couldn't stop it. "Hi, I'm Cathy," I heard my voice chirp. "Let's be friends." I opened my eyes to see the little girl smiling down at me.

"Mommy," she said excitedly. "Let's buy this poor old dolly. She can still talk."

GRAVE SECRET
By Donna Leach

Billy rested the barrel of his rifle on top of the fencepost and took aim. "Okay, Joseph, let him loose."

Joseph knelt and sat the large rabbit on the ground. The cottontail stretched his neck and nibbled on a dandelion. Joseph scurried over the fence and stood next to his older brother. "What are you waiting for? Shoot it."

"It isn't hopping away. The stupid thing is just sitting there."

"Shoot him anyway."

Squinting one eye, Billy drew a bead on the rabbit. He rested a finger on the trigger, took a breath and waited for the rabbit to race off. The cottontail looked up at the boys and wiggled his whiskers.

"Dang it, Joseph," Billy sighed. "Shuck a rock at the ignorant thing and get him running. I can't shoot it while it's sitting there smiling at me ... just ain't sporting-like."

"Who cares?" Joseph grunted. "Pa said to get one out of the pen, kill it, and dress it for supper."

"I know, but I need some target practice. There's a traveling carnival over in Rally, and I hear tell they got a marksman that can hit the bulls-eye dead center at a hundred yards. That's what I'm aiming to do too. I ain't cut out to be a farmer like you and Pa. I want to travel the world performing in a carnival. Now, throw a stone at the critter so I can shoot him on the run."

Joseph bent and picked up a pebble. "Ya'll get now," he hissed as he tossed the pebble at the rabbit.

The rabbit took a hop and stopped to graze on a patch of tall grass.

"That rabbit is dumb as heck," Joseph said. He pulled a slingshot from his rear pocket. "I'll get him going this time." Joseph found a good-sized rock, loaded the slingshot, pulled back on the bands and let go.

The stone rocketed at the prey and struck the rabbit in the head, knocking him off his feet. The cottontail lay on its side motionless.

Billy dropped his finger from the trigger and glanced at his brother. "Why did you have to hit him so hard? I think you killed him."

"Sorry," Joseph said. "I guess I misjudged my strength."

Billy crawled over the fence and lifted the lifeless rabbit by his hind feet. "Yep, he's dead all right. Hey, was this Charlotte's rabbit, Whiskers?"

"I don't know. They all look alike to me."

Billy approached the fence. His eyes narrowed as he held the rabbit out. "See that patch of black fur on his head. That was Charlotte's pet bunny. She's gonna have a fit."

Joseph stuffed his slingshot into his back pocket. "How was I to know? She shouldn't have put him in the same pen with the eatin' rabbits. You suppose that's why he didn't make a run for it when I set him free?"

"Yeah, she had him tamed from runnin' off," Billy said. "Here, you killed it, you clean it." He dropped the cottontail at his younger brother's feet.

A slight smile creased Joseph's lips. "Nailed him on my first shot."

"Billy," Charlotte yelled from behind the barn. "Where's my rabbit?"

Billy glanced at Joseph. "I'm going hunting. You deal with Charlotte."

Joseph knelt and quickly bound the rabbit's legs together with a strip of leather and fastened it to his belt. "I'm coming with you. Charlotte will beat the tar out of me if she sees me skinning her pet."

The boys walked through the overgrown pasture to the stream where Joseph skinned and gutted the rabbit. Afterward, the brothers went into the woods.

A chill was in the air as the fall season replaced the long summer. The boys punched each other on the shoulders to see who was stronger as they scouted the forest looking for game. They came across wild pig tracks. "I wish I had Pa's Winchester with me," Billy said. "I have a mind to hunt down one of those pigs."

"Grandpa Joe would be mighty proud of us if we brought home a pig for the smokehouse," Joseph said. "We better bring something home 'cause Pa's gonna be mad that we ran off all morning and left our chores."

Billy pointed to the ground at other tracks left in the soft dirt. "Turkey," he whispered. "That's almost as good as a pig."

Joseph nodded and picked up a couple of rocks for ammunition to use in his slingshot. "Are you really gonna join the carnival and travel around the country?"

Billy adjusted one suspender across his shoulder. "Yup. I've got a mind for adventure. Milking cows and plowing dirt ain't no life for me. I want to see big cities and maybe sail across the ocean to Egypt and explore the Pyramids. Or go on a safari in India, hunting tigers from the back of a big old elephant."

"What about the family farm? Since you're the first born, you know you're supposed to take over when Pa dies," Joseph said.

"I don't know who made up those dumb traditions, but all I see here is a life of back-breaking work. No thank you, sir. You can have this old place if you want it. I'm planning on catching up with the carnival when they pull out of Rally."

"Pa and Ma ain't never gonna agree to letting you join the carnival. You're just day-dreaming, Billy," Joseph snickered.

"Well, maybe I won't tell neither one of them. I'll just sneak off in the middle of the night, how about that?"

"Boy, oh boy, Pa would skin you alive when he caught up with you." Joseph let out a whistle.

They followed the turkey tracks deeper into the woods until they heard a gobbling sound. The boys cut across a shallow ravine and saw a hen pecking at the ground in the distance. Billy whispered to Joseph, "She's mine."

"Not if I get her first," Joseph whispered back

The boys separated and Joseph crept through bushes until he was a few yards from the hen. He stretched the bands of his loaded slingshot back as far as he could. When he released the rock, he heard a blast from his brother's rifle.

****

Joseph noticed his reflection in the window pane from the side of the house as he approached the back porch carrying the turkey. Mud and blood stained his shirt and pants. He wiped his dirty hand across his shirt, trying to clean up a little before his mother saw him.

Grandpa Joe was sitting in a rocking chair on the porch whittling on a piece of hickory. The old man glanced up when the boy stepped onto the porch. "Well, now fancy that," he said. "You gonna tell me you killed a turkey with your slingshot?"

"Yes sir."

"Where's your brother?" a stern voice barked from behind Joseph.

He turned to see his father limping up the porch steps. "I don't know, Pa."

"I sent you two down to fetch a rabbit from the pen for supper. Charlotte's been crying all morning over her rabbit gone missing. I see a dressed buck hanging off your belt, so which one of you killed it?"

"We fetched a rabbit just like you told us, Pa. Billy wanted to target practice, but the stupid thing wouldn't run, so I popped him with a rock to get him moving."

"So you killed him with a rock, did ya?"

Joseph hung his head and nodded slightly. "But I didn't know it was Charlotte's pet. She shouldn't have mixed him in with the eatin' rabbits."

"Look what else this great hunter killed using his slingshot," Grandpa Joe said proudly and pointed at the hen dangling at Joseph's side. "Hank, you can't get mad at the boy for providing meat for the family table."

"You two had a mind to go off hunting instead of helping with the farm work today?" Hank asked.

"Yes sir," Joseph answered, his head still lowered, staring at his muddy shoes.

"While you were out romping through the woods having yourselves a grand old time, guess who was doing all the chores."

"Sorry, Pa." Joseph felt his heart pumping faster as he looked up into his father's dark eyes.

Hank lifted his hat and wiped his forehead with the back of his hand. He gazed out across the pasture at the woods and dropped his hat back in place. "Take the rabbit in to your ma, and then get cleaned up."

"Yes sir," Joseph said.

"I'll take the turkey," Grandpa Joe said as he stood. "It's a fine kill, Joseph."

Joseph handed the hen to his grandfather. Normally, such a prize turkey would make him feel proud, but he found no joy in the moment. Joseph opened the kitchen door, and upon seeing his mother, tried to kick some of the dried mud off his shoes before entering.

His mother sat at the kitchen table peeling potatoes. "Well, it's about time," she said when she saw the skinned rabbit on Joseph's belt. "I was beginning to think we were going to have vegetable soup for supper instead of rabbit stew." She glanced at the dirt and blood stains on his clothing. "What in tarnation have you been doing? Those clothes are ruined."

Charlotte stomped into the kitchen. "There you are, you little killer. Is that my rabbit?"

Joseph stepped back and avoided eye contact with his sister. He was a year-and-a-half older than her, but she was taller than him, meaner than a wolverine and as strong as an ox. She could whip either of her brothers any day of the week.

Charlotte grabbed a handful of her brother's shirt and twisted it around her knuckles. "You killed Whiskers, didn't you?"

Joseph tried to pull away.

"That's enough, Charlotte. Let your brother be," her mother scolded. "Go fetch the laundry in from the line."

Charlotte released her grip and shoved Joseph backwards. She shook her finger at him. "If you killed my rabbit, I ain't ever gonna forget it." She spun around and her braided pigtails whipped across Joseph's cheek as she marched off.

Joseph unfastened the rabbit from his belt and laid it on the counter.

"Joseph," his mother said. "If that is Charlotte's bunny, you don't tell her. Better for her to think it ran off. What's done can't be undone now, but next time, consider who you might be hurting beforehand."

"Yes ma'am," he answered as he left the room.

After Joseph changed out of his filthy clothes and washed up, he sat on the edge of the bed and stared at Billy's Sunday boots in the corner. He wished his brother was here now. Everyone was mad at him except Grandpa Joe, but that was usually how it went in this house. Ma favored Billy, and Charlotte was the apple of Pa's eye. His mother's advice rung through his head, "What's done can't be undone now, better for her to think it ran off." Joseph hid in his room the rest of the afternoon, his heart heavy with guilt over what he did and for the lies he was about to tell.

His bedroom door swung open before sundown. "Ma sent me to fetch you to supper," Charlotte said. She stared at him like a hawk about to swoop in for a kill. "You can sit in here hiding from me, Joseph, but you can't hide from God. He knows what you did."

Joseph stood. "I didn't kill your dumb old rabbit."

"Then where is he?" she asked.

"How should I know?"

"I put Whiskers in the pen with the other rabbits so he could play with them."

Joseph approached the doorway. "Maybe he found a way out and escaped."

Charlotte stared into his eyes without blinking. "You're lying. Your nostrils always flare when you're fibbing to Pa, and they're flaring now."

"You're dumb," Joseph scoffed as he pushed on by her.

Billy's chair remained empty when the family gathered for the evening meal.

"Where's your brother?" his mother asked.

Joseph took his seat. "I don't know."

His mother passed the bowl of rabbit stew around the table, followed by a pan of biscuits. "Does anyone know where Billy is?" she asked.

Hank glanced over at Joseph. "How come Billy didn't come home with you?"

Joseph swallowed hard. "I told Billy we best get back home, but he found some pig tracks and lit out after them. I knew you'd be powerful mad at us for going off hunting and neglecting our chores and all, but Billy wouldn't listen to me." Joseph glanced around the table. He saw Charlotte staring at his nostrils. He rubbed his nose with the back of his hand, trying to keep his nostrils from flaring under his sister's glare.

"What on earth was he thinking? He knows he needs my Winchester to hunt pigs," Hank said.

"He was just gonna track em and find out where they root," Joseph added quickly.

"Why didn't you tell me this earlier? He should have come home by now," his father said.

Joseph shrugged his shoulders and spooned stew into his mouth, even though he didn't feel much like eating.

Charlotte stirred the spoon around in her bowl, tears welling in her eyes.

"Charlotte," her mother snapped. "Eat your supper."

She looked up at her mother. "I can't do it. I know Joseph's lying. You can't make me eat Whiskers."

Grandpa Joe dipped a biscuit in his stew and took a bite. "Well, pet or no pet, this is mighty good stew. You don't know what you're missing."

Charlotte dropped the spoon in her bowl with a clang. "This is your fault," she yelled at her grandfather. "If you hadn't taught the boys how to hunt, they wouldn't run around killing animals all day." She pushed away from the table and stood. "You turned them into killers. I wouldn't be surprised if Joseph killed Billy too."

"Charlotte Ann," her mother exclaimed, "That's quite enough from you, young lady. Go to your room at once."

Charlotte stormed from the room.

Joseph sat with his mouth open, stunned at his sister's outburst. His family stared at him, waiting for a response. Joseph cleared his throat. "I recall Billy talking about a traveling carnival over in Rally that had a marksman performing for the crowds, and how he wanted to join them and travel the world."

His mother gasped. "You don't suppose he ran off to Rally to join the circus?"

"That's just nonsense, Annie," Hank said.

"Is it?" Annie asked. "You expect two young boys to work this farm and feed the entire family. That's a lot of responsibility."

Hank pushed away from the table. "If I hadn't been run over by that wagon and busted my hip, I'd still be providing for my family without the boys' help."

"I don't mind," Joseph blurted out. "I like hunting and doing chores around the farm. It don't bother me none, Pa."

"I'm going into the woods and fetch Billy home," Hank said as he rose from the table.

"Now Hank," Grandpa Joe said. "The last thing the family needs is for you to be stumbling around out there and maybe bust your other hip as well. Joseph and I will go."

Joseph looked up at his grandfather. "It'll be getting dark soon, Grandpa."

"We'll take a kerosene lantern with us. You show me where you last saw Billy and if he's out there, I'll find him. I used to be the best tracker this side of the Rockies. I'll bet you didn't know that?"

****

"I think we spotted the turkey on the other side of this ravine," Joseph said.

Grandpa Joe lowered the lantern and studied the ground as he walked. He came to a halt. "Did you two boys split up from here?"

"Yep, I went off that way." Joseph pointed to his left.

"That means these tracks belong to Billy," Grandpa Joe said. He followed the tracks that veered to the right.

"I lost sight of Billy from here on," Joseph said.

Grandpa Joe walked slowly ahead, carefully stepping over a tree limb lying on the ground. "Uh-oh," he grunted.

"What?" Joseph asked.

"The tracks are gone. Looks like the dirt's been disturbed." He lifted the lantern and fanned it out in a circle, walked a few more steps, and then knelt and touched the ground. Grandpa Joe rubbed his fingers together and looked at his hand under the light before glancing up at Joseph. "There's dried blood on the ground." He stood and scouted the area.

A lump formed in Joseph's throat. He remained next to the downed limb and watched his grandfather.

Grandpa Joe walked back to Joseph and leaned against the tree. "Now, you told your pa that Billy lit out to follow some pig tracks after you killed the turkey, and that's when you came home, right?"

Joseph nodded.

Grandpa Joe rubbed his chin. "That ain't exactly what happened though, is it?"

Joseph felt his heart racing in his chest. He shook his head.

"From the signs on the ground, I have a good idea about what happened out here. But, you need to come clean with your old grandpa so we can figure this thing out."

Tears welled in Joseph's eyes. "I'm not sure what happened, Grandpa. I aimed the slingshot and released the bands. The rock hit the hen and I heard the gun fire right after. I ran over and saw Billy lying on the ground back here. I think the rock might have ricocheted off the turkey and hit Billy causing him to fall on the rifle."

Grandpa Joe laid his hand on Joseph's shoulder. "No, boy. Billy tripped over this branch, fell, and accidentally shot himself. It wasn't your fault."

"Oh, Grandpa," Joseph sobbed. "The bullet entered under his chin and went straight up into his head."

Grandpa Joe's voice quivered, "What did you do with his body?"

Joseph pointed toward a pile of boulders further down the ravine. "I buried him and the .22 next to those boulders where the ground is soft. I piled rocks over the top to keep varmints from disturbing him. I didn't know how to tell Ma and Pa when I got home. Charlotte was so mad about her stupid rabbit. Then Ma told me to just let her think it ran off. So, I thought maybe it would be better for them to think the same thing about Billy." Joseph peered up into his grandfather's face. "I know they favored Billy, him being the first born. I don't think Ma could stand knowing he was dead, it'd be too hurtful. You're not gonna tell em the truth, are ya?"

Tears trickled down the old man's cheek. He pulled a kerchief from his pocket, dried his eyes, and then blew his nose. "Maybe running off to join the carnival would be a better loss for them to bear." He walked up the ravine and inspected the burial spot. "Did you say a prayer over the grave?"

Joseph nodded. "I gave him a proper burial, Grandpa."

Grandpa Joe looked down at Joseph. "After this night, we'll not speak of what really happened here. Billy ran off with the carnival. You'll have to fill his shoes now. Are you up to it?"

"Yes sir," Joseph said.

"Boy, I'm warning you though, this kind of secret is the kind you can't ever tell; these are grave secrets. Do you understand?"

Joseph nodded, "I think so."

"Let's go home," Grandpa Joe said.

****

The next few days Joseph worked doubly hard on the farm to make up for Billy being gone. The tension in the house was nearly unbearable. Joseph's parents constantly made remarks blaming each other for Billy running off. Charlotte held a grudge about her missing pet, and an uncomfortable silence blanketed the dinner table that week.

Joseph wondered if maybe it was a mistake to keep the secret from his family. If his parents had a chance to grieve Billy's passing, perhaps in time, things would get better. However, Joseph couldn't take the chance that the truth might drive his family further apart.

Annie stared at Billy's empty chair during Sunday supper and dabbed her eyes with her napkin. "I hope my boy is getting enough to eat, wherever he is tonight."

"I'm sure he is," Grandpa Joe said. "No need to fret about Billy. That boy will do just fine on his own."

Hank glanced across the table. "I asked around about the carnival that passed through Rally last week. Preacher Shoemaker said he recalls seeing a boy looking a lot like Billy leave with the carnival when they pulled out."

"See there," Grandpa Joe said. "Just like I told you, the tracks in the forest were headed straight for Rally." He stole a glance at Joseph and nodded. "Ain't that right, Joseph?"

"Yes sir," Joseph answered. "I bet he'll become a famous marksman and live in a mansion in a far away land. And one of these days Billy will probably come marching back up our road, bragging about all his adventures."

"I believe you're right," Grandpa Joe said.

Joseph glanced at his ma and pa. They both had a proud glow on their face. Joseph knew then what his grandfather meant about grave secrets, he had to take this secret with him to his grave.

And so the tradition each evening from then on was to imagine what great places Billy was visiting next. Everyone joined in the discussion at supper time except Charlotte. She refused to participate. After a while, Joseph almost started believing that Billy really was traveling around the country.

One early spring morning, Annie received a postcard from New York City. The sender didn't sign their name, but simply wrote they were having a wonderful time. She swore it had to be from Billy.

Charlotte, being the skeptic of the family, was convinced the postcard was delivered to the wrong address. She held on to her suspicions that Billy died that horrible day many years ago when her bunny disappeared, but she never brought it up again.

Joseph kept the secret, even after Grandpa Joe and both his parents had passed away. Every once in awhile, he'd sneak off into the woods alone and sit next to the boulders in the ravine and talk to his brother.

ALONE

By Winnie Enloe Furrer

The gray sod house stood on a treeless knoll. Smoke above the chimney told me someone was home. There were no animals, not even the usual farm dog. A plow lay at the edge of the field, but had yet to knead the farmland for planting.

I shouted *hello*, but there was no response. My mare came to a halt in front of the house. The door swung open and a short, square-faced woman stood framed in the doorway. Four half-dressed children peeked around her. The long rifle she held across her large breasts accented her seriousness.

"Good morning, ma'am," I said. "My name's Walter. Me and my ride, Sassy, sure could use some water." She made no reply. She stared into my eyes and closed the door.

As I was tying Sassy, the door opened, bringing the aroma of hot coffee and warm flat bread. While the children carried out the vittles, she stood in the doorway. Still holding the rifle, she pointed to the bench next to the well as a resting place. The silent children gathered around her like chicks to a hen. They seemed about to retreat into the house again.

Sensing her uneasiness, I gave her an encouraging smile and said, "We both really needed that water. Thanks. Nice home you have, ma'am. It sure gets lonesome on the trail. I'd be pleased if

135

you and the children would sit a spell." She had no way of knowing how much I longed to hear female chatter about children, chores, and family. "I miss family. I miss hearing voices. It's seems like a mighty long time since I've heard another human voice. I'd love to hear you all talk a mite."

She hesitated. Brushing a strand of dirty, dark hair from her face, guarded eyes met mine. I felt her appraise me from head to toe.

"Ain't talked to no one 'cepting the young'uns for over two weeks," she said.

"Has your husband gone to town?" Again she hesitated, glanced at me, and dropped her gaze to the ground.

"Gone for seed," she said. "He took the dog to keep him company on the trip." She again surveyed the dust.

"I know how much company an animal can be."

"How long you been traveling?" she asked, still testing.

"I've been on the trail about three weeks. I'm headed for Texas." As I finished my bread, we lapsed into a silence broken only by the song of prairie quail.

Never taking her eyes from me, she set the butt of the big rifle by her foot. "What are ya searching for, or running from?"

As I tried to conjure up an answer which would put her at ease, I brushed the trail dust from my old gray hat and said, "I don't know what's in front of me, and no one's chasing me. I guess I just like to see new country and meet new people. I've met quite a few on this trip.

"The spread I was working for in the Dakotas folded. I hear Texas wants good hands and I'm a good wrangler." She seemed pleased with my answer. Her plain face relaxed a little, but she still watched me sip my cooling coffee.

"It gets lonesome here too, cooped up with the little ones makes you feel loony after a while. Don't get much company. Been over two years since I seen another woman." The fields stood barren under her gaze. "But a woman can't be too careful out here, you know."

I nodded. Her eyes suddenly burned with anger and I felt her bitterness. It seemed she had a need to talk and I wanted to listen. She again searched my face, paused, breathed deeply, and slowly started her story.

"Mister was gone. It was nigh on to six months ago, just before winter set in. I didn't have Baby Bo yet, just these four. It was cold and chips dwindled fast. Mister planned to bring some back." She hesitated, attempted to smile, and continued. "He always said he'd bring me the makings of a new dress if he had money left." The small smile left her face. "He's a good man ... works hard ... only gets to see his friends once or twice a year. Can't blame him for wantin' a few drinks and a good time. Anyhow, the money was gone and so ... no new makings. I wasn't really expecting it. Ain't had one since I been here. Young'uns could use a few things though."

I hadn't noticed until she mentioned her clothing that her dark dress was a mass of mending. It had been torn badly again and again. I had no trouble seeing that three of these four children were boys because none wore bottoms. I reckon that's right convenient.

She looked lovingly at each of them. "Well, as I was saying, a woman can't be too careful. It's easy to tempt a man what's been on the trail. The stranger was the first man I'd seen, other than Mister, in almost a year. Never meant to tempt no one." Her fingers tore at a scrap of cloth from her pocket. "I just greeted him at the door and offered coffee."

She stopped and looked at her bare feet a while. As she continued, her voice was a strained whisper. "He tore my dress and bruised me all over. Young'uns was screaming. He was a big brute. I guess I'm lucky I didn't lose Baby Bo. If I'd had the gun then, I'd a killed him."

Her eyes still burned with her pent-up anger. Taut and sober, she gazed at the horizon with her broad brow furrowed. She whispered, "I hate it out here … alone."

Her voice was again strong as she glanced at me and said, "My bruises were almost healed up and the soreness was gone before Mister came home. I weren't gonna tell him. But the young'uns told him about it in their way. I don't hold no grudge. They didn't know what he'd do.

"I can still see Mister's green eyes blazing at me. I knew he was gonna beat me again." Her eyes became red and moist with memory. As her eyes lowered, her voice got soft, "He almost killed me. He wouldn't quit. He just kept swinging … hitting me over and over. He yelled how evil women tempt men … and that Enola here would grow up to be just like me."

There was a long silence as she touched the children's heads and searched the land. She whispered, "I never knew I was evil." Tears still clung to her cheeks when she squared her shoulders, and stood to her full height. "He's a good man. He always says he's sorry."

She suddenly looked at me with almost startled eyes and said, "Lands! Here I am telling a total stranger things I ought not to tell no one. I had no cause to talk your ear off."

"Quite all right, ma'am. Everyone needs to talk out their problems so they can get on with living. Sometimes it's easier to talk to a stranger. Besides, it's been a long time since I've had a chat with a nice lady." I met her gaze and smiled.

She looked pleased. "I'd better get to the chores."

I thanked her, patted little heads, and rode off.

The long, lonely journey gave me lots of time to think about her and her brood. With no family of my own, I found myself worrying about them alone out there, so when I headed north, I knew I would visit their sorry sod house again.

It was late August the next year before I hit the prairie and headed for my home ground.

As the house came into view, the dark summer storm clouds hung low over the prairie. Her home looked smaller and shabbier. I shouted my arrival and again received no response. As I stepped down from my horse, the door opened. The eldest boy stood in the doorway with the rifle held in his small thin arms. I thought him to be about eight.

"Where's your ma?"

"Gone. She's been gone fer months."

"Where'd she go?" I asked in surprise.

"Pa buried her," he mumbled.

I asked if she had taken sick and he responded, "She was sick fer 'bout a week after Pa whipped her the last time he came home."

The little girl peeked under her brother's arm. He smiled down at his sister. "He whipped Enola too, but she didn't go away." When I made no reply he added, "He said he was sorry."

The young boy shrugged his narrow shoulders when I asked him about his paw's whereabouts. He finally said, "Probably in town."

"You want some coffee?" he suddenly asked with a smile as he leaned the rifle against the well. Not waiting for an answer, he turned and ordered, "Enola, get the man some coffee. Sit a spell and talk, mister. We ain't heard no grownup talk for nigh over a week."

The Cusp of a California Spring
By Lianne Card

Back East it's minus 51 degrees.
Record breaking lows, commentators claim.
A woman dies
shoveling snow in her driveway.
Twelve-foot high waves crash off Great Lakes;
traffic pileups jam the interstates.

No snow here.
Nevertheless, I plow through
my inner landscape, clear drifts of paper
clogging my office.
Receding Christmas leftovers
like piles of aging snow, languish
in corners of each room
forgotten ornaments, cookie tins,
gifts not yet put away.

After a brooding fog
spring will descend–
in a blizzard of blossoms:
nectarines, plums, cherries and peaches
will shout their splendor to buzzing bees.
Highway '99 will become
a gossamer fairyland, pink and white.
Pollen will dust my car each morning.

Popcorn flowers, like a sprinkling of snow
will sprinkle green hills
flanking Dry Creek Road
reminding me of snowdrop crocuses
that poke through honeycomb drifts
on Victorian lawns in Canada.

Leaves from the Valley Oak

The desert will bloom in Death Valley.
As the psalmist described in biblical times,
earth and man will rejoice
in spite of wars, and rumors of war.

On my walks I now spy buds.
Clusters of paper whites,
fragrant in a corner of a neighbor's garden,
push up though last year's leaves.
They know how to be nourished
by what was left behind.
Absorbing this life force, they bloom
irrepressible, one more time.

Almost Memorial Day: Tulare County Crop Report
By Lianne Card

After a long spring,
navel orange season winds down;
packers ship a few more crates
to Singapore,
Bahamas, China and Japan.

Tractors crisscross fields,
cut and bale alfalfa,
reap winter grains for silage.
Cotton grows well, a second cultivation but
dry soils will need an extra irrigation.

Avocado bloom is done, crop small
because of last year's freeze.
Grapes bud in roadside vineyards;
crews thin vines for air and sunshine –
clusters will yield sweet raisins.

Stonefruit ripens as summer heat arrives.
Apricots, nectarines, cherries, peaches
appear at roadside stands. Farmers cover
berries with mesh so birds can't feast,
or place mylar flags, flickering rainbows
around each field.
Birds will glean when harvest ends.

This land never sleeps, never lies fallow.
Winter, spring and summer merge:
morning chill one day, swamp cooler the next.
Panorama of plenty reminds us while we rush–
we must remember to taste
each fruit in season.

Birders
By Lianne Card

They arrive–
guidebooks at the ready,
dangling binoculars,
eccentric hats a'kilter.
They scan treetops
for silhouettes.
One arc of wing calligraphy
or helicopter swoopings
signifies a sky move;
pinions will reveal
falcon or hawk.

Birders listen
for stereophonic calls;
each warble, croak or trill
identifies a feathered creature
distinctly named.

Birders count,
comparing numbers sighted
this year opposed to last.
Life lists are their trophies:
evidence of
patience and keen eye.

Birders wait lifetimes
for one rare moment:
"Oh yes! Never been seen before this far west,"
they say, one wondrous day when
wingflutter at fifty feet
makes them explorers,
surveying
undiscovered lands.

Alien Corn
By Lianne Card

July, and the corn is tasseling
high as an elephant's eye in the Broadway song.
Adjacent sun-worn barn, abandoned,
collapses upon itself, while
cattle graze nearby among the oaks,
oblivious.

Cows will not eat this corn,
nor any woman grind flour from those kernels.
She will not slap nor char tortillas for her family.
This corn sustains no sacred triad–
of corn, squash or beans,
once blessed by ceremony
crops to nourish empires.
.

Man-made of mutant seed, this corn
will never nurture living things.
Instead, this corn feeds
steel and glass beasts,
hurtling down highways,
hungry for horizons,
insatiable.

Sierra to the Sea
By Lianne Card

Sierra Nevada at my back
beckoning blue Pacific calls,
like a lover promising a tryst.
I head west as stonefruit and citrus in verdant groves
flank Highway 198.
Under Chinese elms, two horses stand nose-to-tail
communing in the shade.
Family farms are tended lovingly
'til sprawl encroaches.

John Muir once marveled
at wildflowers and grasses stirrup high
when he first glimpsed
the valley of the San Joaquin.

Beyond Visalia I bear down
cross truck-clogged Highway 99,
take one more breath before
BIG AG begins –
a dead zone to be crossed.

Unholy stench of factory dairies ahead –
no happy cows in this California,
whatever TV ads may claim,
no pastures of plenty for miserable creatures,
dishonored by profit.
Tule Lake was drained long ago,
by one man's will.
The Cotton King got his 100,000 acres,
displaced ancient peoples, wildlife, marshes –
turned living soil inert and grey.
Across a bleak expanse,
tractors now rumble, prehistoric beasts

churning clouds of noxious dust.
Nearby, Vipers at Lemoore Naval Air Station
stand ready to strike.

I turn along the California Aqueduct to Highway 41.
There egrets pose –
blinding white silhouettes
against brackish green.
Their purity indicts a habitat
they must call home.

At Kettleman City, the canal flows on.
Sold out by a devil's deal the town became
a dumping ground for garbage from LA.
Land shudders from one more assault;
local people tend the truck stop.
Cross Highway 5, that concrete corridor,
all roads lead to Avenal prison.
Finally, the road descends
and I am John Muir once again.

Carizzo Plain spreads majestic –
purple hills frame panorama,
creation's canvas, austere and empty.
I give thanks, breathe deep, greet
smog-free air and skies of blue.
Beyond the plain,
healthy herds roam lazily
midst the ancient oaks
and golden California hills
'til the Bakersfield cutoff.

At Cholame's Jack Ranch café
stands a granite memorial.
James Dean crashed nearby at twilight;
Japanese tourists visit 50 years later,

loving him, forever young.

Vineyards and wineries for twenty miles–
nothing ramshackle in transplanted Tuscany.
Who would have thought –
old cowboys would become
so enamored of the grape?
Chalk hills lie contoured and sensuous
reminiscent of the Rhone, some say,
a thousand foil mirrors glimmer
protecting precious harvest
from hungry birds.
Each winery beckons:
let the traveler taste, how care and sun
with artful cultivation and Salinas aquifer
has made land once only winter farmed
a new *terroir*.

Twenty miles of grapes to El Paso de Robles,
wine country destination now rebuilt
atop earth's restless fault lines.
Mist floats over the Santa Lucia range
where temblors sleep;
final summit stretches green as
zigzagging west to Highway 46,
I hurry to embrace
my waiting shore.
O ! Blue Pacific, my sweet eternal sea,
you are so welcoming –
you never disappoint.

Orange Blossom Junction
By Lianne Card

We arrive to celebrate
at the local roadhouse;
Isaiah, not quite one year old,
walking since last week,
wears his new shoes.
Our table sits at the outer edge
of the vast, rustic dining room.
Far from other diners,
Isaiah toddles across pine floors freely,
disturbing no one.

We walk with him in turns.
His grandfather points out
photos of guitarists
who've played here.
We order, relax into the evening.
A flamenco guitarist arrives,
sets up his microphones.

First strum brings the cavernous space to life.
Isaiah zeroes in, alert to warm sounds,
totters with shaky steps to the corner stage.
Rodrigo's *Concerto de Aranjuez* moves him.
He dances uninhibited, ecstatic,
waving his arms, shakes his head from side to side.
Unsteady on his legs, Isaiah sits,
then spins himself around
like some break dancer on a city sidewalk.
The guitarist smiles, offers his guitar;
Isaiah is allowed to touch the body and its strings.

Isaiah dances for all of us.
His joy buoys our spirits.

Leaves from the Valley Oak

Our hearts are warmed.
The food is good; we share dessert.
A sampler of house-made sorbets:
pomegranate, lemon, plum –
all refreshing.
Ambrosial tastes
conclude the evening.

We drift out to the parking lot.
Above the orange groves
the autumn moon is veiled with iridescent clouds.
Isaiah points up.
The orb, round like the circle of our lives,
golden like the blessings we feel,
reflects our bounteous harvest.

CAT'S MOON
By Arthur Wallace Neeson

part one

I have been in the service of Sir Thomas, Laird of Kell, since my youth. I caught his eye as I was brawling with my brothers in the courtyard. He thought me a likely sort to guard his household. In truth, I grew to be such, and he set me as his night watch. I had some skills as a hunter, and I accompanied him as he walked about his domain. His fields and woods I treated as my own to wander through, from high rocky ridge to tangled glen.

I was out early one morning to hear the cry of dawn upon the wild Scottish hills and breathe the life of the land. The autumn air was crisp, and a touch of frost was still lingering behind the hedgerow when I saw Auld Lachie MacDougall, the laird's coachman, bring round the carriage. Its grand four-in-hand, proud stallions all, was a thrilling sight with their stamping hooves and tossing heads. With joy I scrambled up to sit beside him on the driver's bench.

"Och, now! You be after going with us?" MacDougall said to me. "'Tis no simple ramble through the woods we be doin'. We're off to town."

Just then Sir Thomas hurried out of the manor door and sprang into the carriage. He tapped on the window behind the driver's bench and we were off.

We were almost to the turn of the road by the ridge when we were stopped by a rare uncanny sight. The road ahead was filled with cats. Tabbies and grays and calicoes in all sizes—on the road, in the ditch below the ridge, and on the ridge itself.

And in the center of this mass was a great black cat, large as a deerhound with spiky fur star-flecked, and throat white like a night cloud lit by the moon. Around him an honor guard kept their vigil—eleven braw buck-cats almost as grand as he. Below these, lesser cats gathered as servants and courtiers.

Sir Thomas rapped impatiently on the carriage window. "Why are we stopping?"

"'Tis unco' strange—a grand sluagh o' cats on the road. Happen they be choosing their king. Happen that's him there."

Sir Thomas leaned out the left side window. "That big black one? What a great ugly brute! I'll wager that's the biggest buck-cat in the country. He's got the Devil in his eyes. Part wildcat, I think."

"That be no wildcat. 'Tis a cait-shee."

"A cat-shee?"

"A fairy cat. Some say they be witches in disguise."

Just then the great cat stretched and yawned. Sir Thomas gasped. "Look at the shanks on the beast! He's built for the chase, like a greyhound. He could stretch up and look you in the eye almost, and a demon grin of teeth, those fangs, like daggers." He stared entranced for a moment, then shook himself. "I have no time for this. Drive on through them!"

"I'll give them no hindrance, and they be settling for a king."

"Then drive on the far ditch-side!"

The King Cat never moved as we passed. A hundred cat's eyes stared in silence as we turned the corner and lost sight of them.

Town was a delicious mix of sights, smells and sounds. I stayed close to MacDougall as he made the round of shops and tavern.

The laird's business took longer than he'd expected, and it was dark before he came to collect us at the tavern. There was storm in his step and lightning in his eyes—his day had not gone well.

"Let's be off! The light's past gone."

Auld Lachie didn't look up from his drink, but stared into his cup, as if he could see all the world's wonders there. "It be late. Best we stay the night in town."

"I'll not sleep the night outside the walls of Kell!"

"Midnight will come afore we reach the turn below the ridge. Midnight is the cats' time, and the cats be at their meeting there."

Sir Thomas tossed his scarf over his shoulder and strode toward the door. "Suit yourself! I'm off to Kell!"

"And to Hell anon, I ha' no doubt," MacDougall muttered into his cup.

I left him with his drink for company and followed the laird to his carriage.

"Ah, you're coming, then?" the laird said to me as I climbed up beside him on the driver's bench. "I should have known that a few cats would not scare the likes of you!"

The night turned wild as we drove down the post road. The wind was cold as it whipped through the trees and chased the clouds across the face of the moon. The sound of it was like a living thing, moaning low along the hedgerows and screaming high as it stripped the leaves from the thrashing branches of the trees. The power of the night excited me, but I could see from his bearing that Sir Thomas was on edge and uneasy as he urged the horses on.

It was high midnight as we reached the ridge turn. The ridge itself lay dark and malignant like a cat behemoth of stone crouched by the road. In the night the eye sees terrors hidden by the light of day, and forcing the horses onward beneath that grim shadow was almost more than Sir Thomas could dare. The night had him, I could feel it. A fascination was upon me. Would he go it on, or break and run? The strain of it was tearing him apart. With a curse he shook himself like a dog shakes off the rain. He shouted at the horses and laid into them with the whip. We thundered into the turn at a full gallop.

The cats were there, filling the road like an army from ditch to ditch and up the ridge. The cats' eyes glowed green in the moonlight—save only the guard cats, the buck-cats, their eyes glowed red. Above all, with eyes blazing like lanterns in the night, loomed the King Cat.

The laird did not slow the horses, but stood up with reins in one hand and whipped the horses on. Through the screaming hordes of cats he drove, wielding his whip from side to side.

Again and again they leaped upon the carriage and launched themselves at him, screaming and tearing at him, and he pounding on them with the butt of his whip and flinging them down to the road. How many died with their eyes still blazing hatred at him, I do not know.

part two

Auld Lachie came home the next day on a farmer's cart. He found Sir Thomas and I at our supper in the Great Hall.

"There be a muckle many cats on the road down by the ridge. A muckle many. All dead. And I think you be the cause of it."

"What of it?"

The laird tried to sound unconcerned, but I sensed that he was still shaken from the night before.

"Now the cats are agin' you. They ne'er were for you, but now they're agin' you. T'will be a difference."

After MacDougall went out, Sir Thomas turned to me. "And you? Do you accuse me also?"

It was not my place to accuse or excuse. I kept my peace.

He slumped back in his chair in disgust. "I never know what you think."

I made no answer, but looked him in the eye, as I had every right to do.

He matched my gaze for a moment, then looked down. "Sometimes you put the dread on me."

I spoke no word, but turned away, and stared into the fire.

The next morning the laird came to me in great excitement. "Come with me, I need your help!"

I followed him, intrigued by his exhilaration. He led me to the Great Hall. The Hall was semi-detached from the rest of the Manor, with a grand double door facing south, six arched windows facing east and six west. At the north end a huge fireplace dominated the room. A door to the left of the fireplace gave the only connection with the rest of the mansion. Facing the fireplace was the laird's great chair where he was want to warm himself of an evening.

As was usual on all but unseemly days, all twelve windows were wide open. In the center of the room, the trestle table was still set up from the night before. Around the corner of the table was the wonder that had so excited the laird.

A fawn stood by the cold fireplace.

"Isn't it beautiful? It must have jumped through one of the windows. It doesn't seem old enough. I don't know where its mother is."

I wondered at his animation. In his time, he had killed many a deer. But the relationship between hunter and prey is complex, almost loving.

"Help me to shoo it out the door or back through a window," he said.

Young as it was, it was nimble enough. It led us a merry chase skittering around the chairs and table, going everywhere but where we wanted it to go. Finally we had it cornered on the west side by the fireplace.

From stock-still it leaped high above the sill and out through the window.

In mid-air the King Cat caught it by the neck, killing it instantly.

The terrible beauty of this aerial dance of death shook me. I shall never forget the sight of the magnificent black beast rising like night flung into the face of day, every fiber of his being at full stretch, claws aching in air. The sheer impact was enough to break the fawn's neck, but inch-long fangs sank deep, sundering spine and severing the cord of life. Death was silent, unheralded, almost kind.

All was over in an instant, the air innocent, empty, the day serene.

I looked to Sir Thomas to share the joy of this wildness, but I saw no expression in his face, only a slow draining of color. His nostrils flared and thinned. The corner of his mouth began to twitch, a tremor that spread to his entire frame. No terror there, but a growing, towering fury. He turned without a word and strode to the door beside the fireplace and disappeared within.

I was of a wonder at him, that he acted so strange, and more at his return. He was wearing great chain mail gauntlets from some ancient armor, and had in hand a hefty brass-bound strongbox. He gave neither word nor look to me as he stalked through the hall and out the high doors. I called, but he gave no heed. I ran to catch up with him.

I soon found him, but not he alone. The King Cat crouched before him, growling above his gory prey.

Sir Thomas threw down the strongbox with a resounding crash and flung it open. He turned again to the King Cat and stood motionless, staring. The cat gave no ground, but matched him stare for stare. It was a duel, a duel of glare and hatred.

Then with an oath, Sir Thomas threw himself at the King Cat. It was a terror to see it, and a terror to see the beast spring to meet him. Sir Thomas held nothing back—a monster himself, transformed and terrifying. Long they rolled and roared, monstrous beast against man-monster, claw and fang against chain mail gauntlet.

Then Sir Thomas raised the cat-shee high, hurled him into the strongbox and slammed the lid shut.

He closed the massive steel lock, then with every muscle straining, he lifted the chest. Not many a man could lift that box with what was within it, but the laird was strong, and had the anger on him. He set off across the road and down into the glen.

What he was about, I could not fathom. I called after him. Sir Thomas didn't answer.

A fear came on me. I ran to him, even daring to cut in front of him, but he brushed me aside and ignored my cries.

Down in the wood that fills the hollow there is a loch, no more than a pool, but deep, fed by a small spring. At its edge Sir Thomas stopped and caught his breath for a moment, then heaved the box into the water.

In a frothing maelstrom of bubbles the chest sank. Stock-still in shock, I could not stop this unnatural murder. All I could do was watch as the Cat King drowned.

part three

The moon was riding high that night and the wind moaning coldly beneath the eaves and rattling at the windows as I made my rounds of the drafty corridors.

At the laird's chamber door I heard a shout and was inside in an instant. Moonlight streaming in from the window lit the bed. The laird was sitting upright, his eyes staring. Great shudders shook his frame. At my inquiry, he startled, then relaxed somewhat.

"Oh, it's you. It was only a nightmare. I heard that beast screaming, and I saw his demon eyes."

A dark shadow fell upon him then. Black in the window was the shape of a gigantic cat. The laird leaped in terror from the bed and backed against the wardrobe.

For a moment he stared at the window, then released a shuddering breath. "It is only one of his foul minions. Be gone!" He ran to the window and flung it open, knocking the beast off. He closed the window, making a sound like a strangled chuckle, like a cackle through clenched teeth. He turned from the window—and froze in horror. Wondering, I followed his gaze.

There was a cat on his bed.

It was of ordinary size, but filthy, with matted fur and glaring eyes. It arched its back and hissed at him. From behind the wardrobe another came, leaping to join his comrade. From the corridor two others marched in to take up positions in the corners of the room. All stared with hate-filled eyes at Sir Thomas.

He slept no more that night.

The next day was like a nightmare set loose. Cats were everywhere, hissing from his table and clawing at his ankles from under his chair. They followed him from room to room constantly watching, watching.

MacDougall joined us, but could give no comfort.

At last Sir Thomas leaped from his chair. A dozen cats snarled. At the door the laird turned to us and shouted, "I canna bear it na mair!" His lapse from the English shocked me to a knowledge of his state.

MacDougall tried to calm him. "Now, now, where you be off to, in such a rush?"

"To set the hounds on these vermin!"

"Och, well, 'twill be the ructions, that."

Ructions it was that day, the Devil's serenity indeed. From howl to yowl, from barn to bale, the brawl went on, fang and fur and claw in bloody battle. The two hounds, great cruel beasts that roamed my earliest nightmares, ran them like rabbits, shaking one and slinging it aside to take another in their well-fanged jaws. The cats in turn with horrid hisses and slashing claws, fought back.

All went the dogs' way until they cornered a crew of cats by the garden wall. They were closing in to kill when from the top of the wall sprang two of the great buck-cats. The dogs went down, and with the witch-cats on their backs and the rest tearing at their sides, they were in for it. They shook off the cait-shees and fled down the lane.

Sir Thomas stumbled into the great hall. "My poor hounds! But the brave lads have bought me a time of peace at least, for every foul mange is chasing after them." He collapsed into his chair by the fireplace.

MacDougall shook his head. "Not every one. Not the chieftains, the grand buck-cats. Tonight be the Eve of Summer-wane, the last full moon of summer, the Cat's Moon. They be going to the burning place to mourn their King."

"I did not burn him. I drowned him in the mere."

"You dinna burn him! You dinna burn him! Are you daft?" Lachie's voice was a shuddering whisper. He was called Auld Lachie, but now he seemed to age before my eyes. He held out a trembling hand and touched the laird's face with some trace of forgotten affection. "I mind when you were a wee bairn. You were such a braw lad, such a bonnie braw lad." He had the sadness on him then, as he turned and slowly left the hall.

The laird watched him go, then murmured softly, "Would that you had struck me, you blethering old bodach."

part four

For a while we sat in silence, save only for the crackling of the fire as the turf-sod shifted on the hearth. All the windows were yet wide open, and the chill of the dying day stole the warmth from the flames.

The laird had a quietness, a weariness about him, but I could not keep still. Something in the atmosphere touched my nerves. A sudden eerie wail brought me to my feet, spine rigid, every fiber tight stretched, listening.

"Peace, my friend," Sir Thomas said to me. "It is only the wind, skirling in the trees."

I could not calm myself, but began pacing. The hall was lit yellow-red by the lowering sun. I could see through the open windows long shadows like bars stretching from every tree and post.

I stopped, frozen in my tracks, every nerve on edge at the sound of screams like distant demons calling me.

"Softly, softly," the laird said, "it is only the cries of the wild geese passing."

I took no heed, but turned and was out and off. I heard Sir Thomas calling me, but I could not bide.

I was drawn to the hollow, and the dark pool at its heart. On its moldering banks, a weirdness came upon me, an ominous waiting, and I felt in the air about me a feverish anticipation.

The sun sank bloody red on that Hell's Eve as I began my vigil. Dark shadows crept around me, and the night wind made strange murmurings through the rushes.

Then darker shadows slipped through the moonlight to the water's edge.

Cats. Black cats, huge as hounds, with wild glowing eyes. I felt their presence more than I heard their approach as one by one they took their places. None of them looked at me, only stared unblinking at the dark, cold waters.

The lake was still, untouched by the chilling breeze above it, reflecting like a silver mirror the bone white trees on the far shore.

A single bubble surfaced, sending a small wavelet out in an ever-widening circle like an opening eye.

The cats around me crouched closer to the water. A hectic thrill mounted in my chest, tingling like a limb awakened from sleep.

The water now was frothing, boiling like a battle was being waged in the dark depths below.

Like a leviathan leaping from the deep, a huge dark shape broke free from the waters.

On the pond's moss-damp shore, his skin hanging gray-rotted, ragged, his fur slimed and matted, stood the Cat King. Bloated by his stay with Death, no hound of Ireland could be as huge, and no demon fresh from Hell's sulfurous breast could glare with such fire in his stare.

Coughing phlegm and slime from his bubbling, decaying lungs, he took breath and yowled forth his challenge call. The sound of it has not been heard on earth before, and shall not be heard again until the gates of Hell are burst asunder upon the Last Day. Screaming high and slashing low, like a scimitar sundering soul from sound and sight, like a beast itself, it rose rampant in the night. Its timbre thrilled me, maddened me, shook me.

Like a chorus of demon song, all on the shore answered his call.

Then the Cat King turned his fire-eyes uphill, toward the Manor. He growled, a deep, guttural thunder, like a roar still holding in his throat. All took up the war talk, and surged with him up the slope.

Heart pounding, I leaped ahead of them, bounding up the path, reckless in my headlong rush.

The great high doors of the hall were shut, like twin sentinels barring entrance. But I was born here, and knew every twist and byway. I turned corner to the western side of the hall. There the windows were open still, six on the west to match the six on the east. I sped past five and jumped up on the broad sill of the sixth.

The hall was lit from the blaze in the great fireplace. Sir Thomas was in his high-backed chair, but contrary to his usual manner he was facing away from the fire, toward the great high doors.

He looked up and gave me a weary smile. "Ah, you've come to warn me. No need. I heard his horrid yowl. I know it well, it echoes from my nightmare. He's coming for me, to judge me—and here is my jury!"

One by one, the Conjure Cats, the Witch Cats came. One by one, window by window, until in every window a hulking black shadow loomed.

All was silence, save only the crackling of the fire. Then with a thunderclap roar the high doors burst open.

The Cat King stalked in to complete the unlucky number.

Up on the table he leaped, almost breaking it beneath his fetid weight. For a moment he snarled down at the laird, then nodded once to the left and once to the right. The Conjure Cats crouched, ready to spring.

Sir Thomas stood up and threw off his cloak. He was clothed in a full coat of chain mail. In one hand he held a club and in the other he held a dagger.

They were on him then, the Witch Cats, the Conjure Cats. The battle raged beneath the Cat King's gaze. With tooth and claw they tore at him, and he at them with club and knife.

Half a dozen of the demons were down, and the laird untouched, when the Cat King's strangled screech froze us all. The Witch Cats fell back, leaving the field to their King. With a gurgling growl he leaped upon Sir Thomas, clamping fore-claws and jaws on the laird's head.

In that gruesome grasp Sir Thomas staggered back. Ten hind talons tore the gauntlets from his arms and shredded the chain mail from his chest. Belly ripped open and ribs flayed bare, he fell at my feet and lay there in agony, the Cat King vulture-crouched upon his breast.

Sir Thomas raised his bloody gaze, beseeching me to break my neutrality.

I looked to my King to give me grace, and with mine own claws, I slashed the eyes from our enemy's despairing face.

THE SHIMMERLING
By Arthur Wallace Neeson

Gregory Harridge was a boy who feared the sea, so he pretended to love it and begged his father to buy him a small sailboat. He learned to sail it in the bay near his family's new home on the west coast of England, then ventured out along the coast beyond the bay. After a while, he forgot to be afraid and began to truly love the swell of the ocean and the wild salt smell of the wind that filled the sail.

He feared many things, but no one ever knew. *Face Fear and shake him by the hand.* It was his motto, though he didn't call it that. He thought of it more as a curse. When he found something that frightened him, he went on with it anyway, and pretended not to be afraid.

That's why he was now crouching, terrified, trapped in a walled garden at midnight.

"You best not be in the lane tonight," the old woman of the village had said. She pointed down to the harbor. "The night wagons be carryin' the souls of the dead to the black ship."

Gregory was puzzled. Sometimes the villagers teased the city boy. "That's just the old Scottish fisherman's boat. It's not black, it's just dirty."

She drew her shawl close about her and shook her head. "An' the fisherman's just a fisherman, but not tonight."

"Tonight?"

" 'Tis the Eve."

"You mean Halloween? It's not for two days."

"The Eve of Summerwane; the waning, the fading, the end of Summer. 'Tis the moon of Summerwane, an' tonight be its fullness. The night wagons come for the souls of those who died the year past, to take them down to the black ship for their passage beyond the Edge, beyond the West. If you stray in the moonlight on the Eve of Summerwane, you might find yourself taken away."

Straying in the moonlight was the last thing he wanted to do, so he knew he had to do that very thing. And now a night wagon was rolling, rumbling ever closer.

The low thunder sound stopped. Gregory peeked out of the garden gate. He hadn't believed it when the old woman said the night wagons carried the dead, but when he saw the black shape trundling into the lane, he hid in the nearest shelter he could find— a walled garden. He tried to shut the gate, but it was stuck. He hadn't realized there was no other way out until it was too late.

The wagon had stopped at a cottage up the lane. The old Scottish fisherman, *the Ancient Mariner* as Gregory thought of him, climbed down from the cart and stood by the cottage gate. He held out his hand.

A glistening smoke, drifting like a cloud of quicksilver star dust, flowed down the path from the doorway.

Gregory shuddered. *That thing is someone's soul.*

The mariner led the shimmering spirit to the night wagon. Gregory could see that the cart held other silvery shadows sparkling in the moonlight. The new soul poured up into the cart.

166

The dark fisherman climbed into his place and urged the two black horses onward.

Towards Gregory.

He gasped and fell backwards, scuttling on heels and elbows into the overgrown shadows of the garden. The rumbling thunder of the cart's wheels rolled closer and closer.

And stopped, right in front of the garden gate.

The ancient fisherman climbed down from the cart. Gregory could clearly see his face in the moonlight, from his lined brow to the floodtide of his grizzled, white-flecked beard. Only his eyes were shadowed, like deep pits. He came into the garden slowly, measuring each tread as if expecting the earth to move with some underground wave. Right in front of the bushes where Gregory was hiding, the fisherman stopped.

He held out his hand.

Gregory almost forgot to breathe. Jammed back in the shrubbery of the garden, he felt like he had become part of it—rooted, frozen to the ground with fear. He couldn't have moved if he had wanted to, and he didn't want to.

The mariner stood like a granite statue in the moonlight with his hand still outstretched. After a long while his voice rumbled deep. "Will ye no come this time, neither?"

Gregory heard something in the old man's voice; it almost sounded like ... sadness.

"It's what must be, it's what ye must do." He dropped his hand to his side. "Ye'll come anon, when ye be ready." He turned and slowly walked back to the night wagon.

This time. He had said "this time, neither." Gregory hated logical conclusions, they always turned out badly for him, but he couldn't stop his mind from churning on. It was as if ... as if ...
as if the fisherman had been speaking to someone else.

Gregory heard the sound behind him then. Knowing exactly what he would see when he turned around didn't lessen the shock and horror. Looming in the moonlight behind him was the shivery, silvery, streaming form of a disembodied soul. Gregory wanted nothing more than to run screaming away, so of course he knew he had to stay rock stock still right there. The flowing gossamers curling in the moonlight were so ... so ...

Beautiful. In finding the word, he lost his fear. He knew that not everything that was beautiful was always good, but there was gentleness in the delicate swirls of the silver smoke-being before him, a gentleness and an innocence.

And life, vibrant life. There was no wind, no breeze in that walled garden; all the graceful movements of the shimmering form were those of a living person. A very small living person, Gregory realized. He was not standing, of course, he was still crouching where he had been hiding, and the child's soul was looming very small in the moonlight.

It was a child, and it was crying. There were no tears, disembodied or otherwise, but Gregory could tell from the tremulous sounds it made, and the shudders that ran through the fabric of its soul.

Sounds? "Can you speak?" Gregory asked gently.

"I don't know." It was a little girl's voice; perhaps he didn't hear a voice so much as a feeling of the words.

"Why are you crying?"

"I'm afraid of going with him. He's come for me twice before."

"You're scared of the old fisherman. Me, too."

"Him? Of course not, he's my uncle!" She was silent a while, then said in a small whisper, "It's the going I'm afraid of."

"But I think you're supposed to go."

"But I don't want to leave. My uncle made this garden for me. I love it. I don't understand why I have to leave."

"I don't think we have to understand, we just have to go."

"But I don't know where I'm going. I'm scared."

"I'm scared of most everything. But I can't act scared all the time, so I pretend I'm brave." He thought a moment, then said, "If I … if I go with you to the ship, will you pretend to be brave?"

The shimmering flicker that was the child's soul was still for a long while, then he heard a whispered, "Yes."

He held out his hand. Her shadows of light melted and flowed and slipped lightly around his fingers. Her touch felt tingly, cool but not cold. He walked with her down to the waterfront.

The black ship was docked there. A glistening shadow in the moonlight, it still had the lines of the fishing boat: sleek, clinker-built and low to the water, with single mast and oarlocks on her gunwales, but in its dark cloud blackness it felt deeper, as if it were bigger on the inside.

The night wagons were standing empty. The last few gleaming shadows were flowing onto the deck of the ship of souls. Dark shadows he took to be sailors were untying the moorings, preparing to cast off.

"Wait!" Gregory's voice was high and shaky. "There's one more."

"You, Lad?" It was the old fisherman. "Y' still ha' flesh about ye."

"Not me," Gregory said quickly, "I brought her." The soul child was hiding behind him.

"Weel, then come along 'board, lass." There was no sadness in his voice now.

The ephemeral glow, the living shadow of the girl, shuddered back. The boy spoke softly to her. "It's what has to be. It's what you have to do."

Gregory bit his lip for a moment, then took a shuddering breath. "It's what has to be," he said again. He turned to the mariner. "Sir, if I go with her, may I come back?"

"Y' ha' flesh. Yer flesh sha' bring y' back. I'm o' quicken flesh as ye."

Gregory turned to the little shimmerling. "Come with me. We'll pretend to be brave together."

He stepped on board the ship of shadows. Once more he held out his hand. Like liquid silk she flowed to him. She hovered close as he walked across the creaking deck to the fisherman.

"Laddie, can ye wield an oar? We must be out some afore we catch the wind."

The boy took the oar from the mariner. "Have you... have you done this a long time?"

"Long as me beard, an' a wee bit more."

"Are there many children?"

"Aye, too many, a muckle much too many."

"Are they ever afraid like her?"

"Some be."

The boy slipped the oar into the oarlock. "If any are afraid, you can stop by my house. I'll go with them." He leaned into the stroke as they passed silently from the shore.

A FUNICULA THING HAPPENED
AT SCHOOL TODAY
By Arthur Wallace Neeson

Butch and Carl were the class bullies when I was in the third grade in Los Angeles. I was a skinny runt of a kid, and they thought I was the most fun to tease. Their favorite thing was to hang me upside down and shake me until I did something they wanted me to do, like dance the *Hokey Pokey*, or give them some of my lunch.

My lunch was a peculiar do-it-yourself thing I put together every morning at the little grocery store on my way to school. My father had set up a kind of charge account there—an open tab that he paid every month. I was a latchkey-kid without a key. I got in the house through a tiny closet window, and I fed myself at the grocery store. I made no great advances in the science of nutrition, but I didn't starve.

I did better in school than Butch and Carl, which was kind of strange, since I often copied from them on tests. I hadn't learned to read, but no one had noticed yet.

After one test, I asked Carl why his was marked *Fail* and mine was marked *Passed*. They were identical.

"She don't want you back in her class next year."

"What about you?"

"She don't care. I've done been held back once. They don't put you back twice."

Our teacher wasn't the most caring person, and I happened to be low on her list of things to care about.

She certainly didn't care if she embarrassed me. When she thought I was taking too long in the bathroom after recess, she sent a girl to fetch me rather than a boy. Everyone was standing around watching when we came out. Teacher had a thin, compressed smile on her face.

I tried to imitate that smile in the mirror, but it hurt too much.

On Friday afternoons our class had music time in the auditorium. We sat in a half-circle on the floor in front of the stage. Teacher thought this was cozy and informal. We thought it was just uncomfortable.

On one of these occasions, Teacher told us to open our songbooks to a page where there was a picture of a train going straight up the mountainside. The words on the page opposite meant nothing to me since I was still stubbornly illiterate. I wasn't paying much attention to what the teacher was saying until she mentioned that it was a 'funicular' railroad.

I instantly blurted out. "I know that song— it's *Funicula*!"

Teacher smiled the way she always did before doing something unpleasant. "Since you know it so well, perhaps you would like to sing it for the class."

She meant to embarrass me, but I loved that song. I jumped up and immediately belted it out. I knew it was an Italian song, so I swaggered through it like I thought a saucy Italian boy would.

> "Some think
> the world is made for fun and frolic,
> and so do I, and so do I!
> Some think

it well to be all melancholic,
to pine and sigh, to pine and sigh.

"But I,
I love to spend my time in singing
some joyous song, some joyous song;
to set the air with music bravely ringing
is far from wrong, is far from wrong!

"Listen! Listen!
Music sounds afar!
Listen! Listen!
Music sounds afar!
Funiculi, funicula! Funiculi, funicula!
Joy is everywhere, Funiculi, funicula!
Hey!"

On that 'Hey!' I knelt on one knee with my hand outstretched in my best showman style.

Butch and Carl loved it. They loved it so much, in fact, that for a whole week they caught me every recess, held me upside down and shook me until I sang *Funicula* for them.

Every class had to do one assembly for the whole school, and our turn was approaching fast. I volunteered to do the curtains. I thought that was fairly safe. All I had to do was yank on a cord.

Almost everyone had something to perform. One boy recited some drivel about a tree. I think he picked it so he could say the word 'breast.'

Teacher looked at me. "Arthur, do you have something to do for the assembly?"

Butch and Carl had been whispering together in the back. Now they shouted out, "Sing *Funicula!*"

"I'm not going out on that stage in front of everybody in school."

Butch and Carl shouted out again. "Sing *Funicula!*"

Teacher smiled that smile I hated. "The girls aren't afraid, why should you be?"

"They can look like idiots if they want to. I'm not."

Now everybody was shouting, "Sing *Funicula!* Sing *Funicula!*"

So I sang *Funicula* for them at the end of every rehearsal, but I made it clear that the only thing I was going to do in the assembly was the curtains.

The day of the assembly everything went off as planned. One by one each act marched on stage and made fools of themselves. I happily worked the curtains.

After the last act, I closed the curtains. I thought we were done, but Teacher signaled me to open the curtains again.

"And now for our final performance," she announced, "Arthur Neeson will sing *Funicula.*"

A scattering of polite applause and then dead silence.

Teacher thought I would feel honor bound to step up and sing out.

Of course, I did no such thing.

What I did do was glare in fury at her. Every muscle in my body tightened as rage shook me.

Head lowered, fists tightened, I was the skinniest bull at bay ever.

Teacher waved wildly in some insane sign language. In answer, I shook my head so hard I came off the floor.

I landed solid, sounding in the silence of the waiting auditorium like a gunshot.

She gave up on me and started signaling to Butch and Carl. They were just behind me shaking with laughter. To them this was the best part of the show.

It was very clear what she wanted them to do.

Push Little Arthur onstage.

Butch looked at me with those teasing eyes of his. I was ready to punch out both of them.

That's when Butch winked at me.

Then he charged— with his hand held out like a tagger in a relay race.

"Swing me."

In shock, I did what I was told. I grabbed his hand and swung him on his way.

Out on to the stage he staggered, arms and legs flailing, knocking the papier-mâché tree down, which in turn knocked the podium to the stage with a splintery, thundery, truly satisfying roar. Butch then flung himself dramatically on top of this magnificent wreckage.

I suddenly knew what *taking a dive* meant.

Butch the Bully on the floor. My Hero.

"It's my turn now," Carl said behind me.

This time I knew what was expected of me and slung him out like a deranged merry-go-round.

Carl stumbled across the stage and straight through the painted backdrop that he had worked on so hard all week. He staggered back, dragging the scenery with him, finally landing with a crash beside Butch.

Splayed out on the floor like the Slaughter of the Innocents, they were the best boys in the world. Maybe the best boys ever.

After school that day I took them to the store and treated them to all the candy and soda they wanted, and I climbed on top of the counter and sang *Funicula* as much as they could stand.

Daddy took my charge account away when he found out, but it was worth it.

Teacher never said anything to me about the show. In fact, I don't think she ever spoke to me again.

'*Funiculi, Funicula*' was written in 1880 by Luigi Denza for the opening of the Mount Vesuvius Funicular Railway. A funicular railway is a cable railway in which the ascending car and the descending car counterbalance each other.

ON THE EVE OF SUMMER-WANE
By Arthur Wallace Neeson

On the eve of Summer-Wane
I heard my true love say
"Alas my love, I leave you now
and in the earth must stay.
Yet as the year does churn around
and cold rains kiss the ground
on the eve of Summer-Wane
I shall return again."

Winter walks into the Spring
and sorrows follow pain.
Summer heals the cold of Spring
but cannot break my chain
and on the eve of Summer-Wane
my true love walks again.

His kiss is cold, and chill his hold
and yet it comforts me.
And on the eve of Summer-Wane
we are lovers free.

THREE MOODS

By Arthur Wallace Neeson

BORDERLAND

i walk a borderland
where wandering sand
and wind-wild wave
wage constant war

yet before
the willing waves
curl and crash upon
the waiting shore
there hangs a moment

when
emerald walls
open crystal windows
upon the deaths
seen deep within

then
the sea

draws me to its caves of wonder
calls me with its waves of thunder
sounds me down to its den of silence

then
the silent sea
retreats
in silent victory

SECOND SIGHT
By Arthur Wallace Neeson

i have left you
my city
you sullen, sluttish
perversity
of concrete

i shed your dirt
your air
is cleansed from me
i forget you
you desert of deceit

no

you breathe too deep
your crowded streets
still haunt me
your desolate humanity
still taunts me

i remember
your hopeless hungers
your drunken alleyways
your dustfilled days
and lustfilled nights

and now
from faraway
i see
a second sight
of sorrow

HAPPY
By Arthur Wallace Neeson

the times are set a-wrong
my love
but they are set
we must now forget
all pain and all regret
and not let mindless surgery
break us now and never mend
let us begin

let there be an end to evil
yet not to love
let not this flower die
though its birth be from a grave
and from this hour
let us save
some small
contentment

and we shall ask for peace
if not for joy
to cease
from sorrow
and together be
in some small part
in some small measure
happy

LARCENY'S REWARD
By Gloria Getman

Dolen Hoskins was enjoying a Sunday afternoon nap when he heard the clatter of metal outside the front screen door. He'd been lying on the couch in the living room of his rented cottage for the last hour dreaming about a new car. The noise roused him, and he knew exactly what had caused it without looking. His cousin, Clarence, had dropped his run-down bicycle against the bricks of the empty planter box outside.

Clarence cupped his hands around his eyes and peered through the screen. "Dolen, she's back." His voice held an element of panic.

Dolen groaned and sat up. He slipped his feet into his flip-flops and shuffled to the door. "Who's back?"

"Claudia's back."

Clarence stepped aside as Dolen unlatched the door and opened it for him.

"Claudia? What the hell is she doing here?"

Before the words were out of his mouth, he thought he already knew. It could mean only one thing. Grand Mama was dying. It was the only reason Claudia would return to Four Creeks.

"What are we gonna do?" The perpetual worry line in Clarence's brow was deeper than usual.

"Nothing. Absolutely nothing."

"But she'll kill us when she finds out what we've done."

"She's not going to find out."

"That's what you think. She's smart. She writes all those detective books. She'll figure out it was us."

"Go home, Clarence."

"But...."

"Go home. I got some thinking to do, and I can't concentrate with you whining."

Clarence stepped out the door. "I'll go, but I wasn't whining. I was just stating the facts. You'll see. She's gonna kill us." He picked up his bike from where it lay on its side and peddled off, mumbling to himself.

Dolen slouched into a nearby cushioned chair. *Claudia. Back in Four Creeks.* He laid his head back and thought of the last time he'd seen Claudia. It had been on the beach at the lake. She'd been wearing a shiny blue bikini that left little to the imagination. He'd watched as she applied suntan lotion to her long legs. Remembering the scene caused a physical reaction. He rose and walked to the kitchenette, opened the refrigerator and pulled out a can of beer. After flipping the tab, he guzzled a sizable amount. *A man shouldn't think about his cousin like that.*

The beer left a bitter taste in his mouth. He set the can on the counter and rubbed his forehead with his fingertips. Clarence was right. Sooner or later Claudia *would* figure out what they'd done — unless he could come up with some diversion. He'd have no trouble with a first-class lie. He'd done that often enough. But Clarence could be a problem. Clarence's mind didn't run along such devious lines. His thoughts were more childlike. Ever since that car knocked him off his bike, it was like he was mentally stunted.

The telephone's ring jarred Dolen out of his meandering thoughts. He reached for the wall phone. Before he even said hello, the high-pitched nasal voice of his ex-wife made his nerves grate.

"Dolen Hoskins, I better find a check in my mailbox this week. You haven't paid me a penny in six months and I've run out of patience. If I don't get a check soon, I'm going to sic the cops on you."

"I told you, Shirley. I got laid off."

"Pfttt. It was your own fault. If you hadn't tried to put the moves on the boss's secretary, you'd still be selling cars."

"How'd you hear about that?"

"Word gets around."

"Never mind. I've got some money coming. When I get it, I'll pay everything I owe."

"You better, and this week. Or else you'll never see your daughter again."

The rude click in his ear made him grit his teeth. *That woman. Divorced five years and I still can't get her out of my life. I could give her the whole eighty grand and she wouldn't be satisfied.*

He poured the remaining beer down the sink, tossed the can in the trash and thought about his little tow-headed daughter. *Poor Mira. She'll grow up to be a witch just like her mother.* He waved his hand as if brushing away cobwebs and turned his attention to his other problem. *I better get over to the nursing home before Claudia has a chance to turn Grand Mama against me.*

As Dolen rounded the corner into the living room, the neighbor's rose garden came into view through the front window. It gave him an idea. He returned to the kitchen and dug around under the sink until he found a vase. After rinsing it, he dried it with paper towels and headed out the front door. Glancing up and down the block of houses, he approached the rose bushes. Luckily, the view from the neighbor's window was blocked by her garage.

Dolen fished a jackknife out of his pocket, sliced free several red roses and plunked them in the vase. After slipping the knife back into his pocket, he glanced around at the neighborhood again before heading to his beat-up Dodge Intrepid in the carport.

As he turned the key, he considered the car. The tires were nearly bald, the radiator had a small crack, and there was only a quarter tank of gas. But at the moment, it would have to do. If his plans worked out, he'd soon have a brand new car.

Valley Oaks Rehabilitation Center sat on the corner of Elm Street and Coral Avenue. Dolen's grandmother, Happy Sidell, had been convalescing there for the last six months following a fall. Dolen had visited once during that time, a fact that wasn't going to set well with Claudia. But he hated places like Valley Oaks. They smelled odd and some of the residents gave him the creeps.

He flashed the twenty-something receptionist a smile as he entered the building and signed the guest log that lay on the desk in front of her.

She glanced at the vase in his hand and then at his name. "The roses are beautiful. Your grandmother will be *so* happy to see you."

"And I'm looking forward to seeing her. She's such a sweetheart. By the way, has my cousin Claudia been here today?"

The receptionist pointed to Claudia's name on the roster and turned her brown eyes up at him like a puppy begging for a bone. "Yes indeed. She was here *all* morning."

"Aw. I'm sorry I missed her." He turned toward the hallway leading to the patient rooms. "You have a good afternoon," he said over his shoulder. *Sheesh. Temptation is everywhere.*

After a few steps, he realized he couldn't remember his grandmother's room number and stepped back in view of the receptionist. "Uh, what was that room number again?"

"Two-o-two."

He flashed her another of his best smiles. "Oh sure, that's right. Thanks."

Glancing at the room numbers as he went, he proceeded down the hall and found Happy Sidell sleeping peacefully in the bed nearest the door. Her face had a translucent quality in the afternoon sunlight. Dolen gave a shudder and stepped to his grandmother's bedside.

He cleared his throat.

Happy didn't rouse.

"Grand Mama?" Dolen said in a firm, clear voice.

His grandmother's eyes snapped open and she looked up at him. "Good gracious, Dolen. You don't have to shout. You almost made me wet my pants. The one thing I have left is my good hearing. Almost too good sometimes."

"I brought you some flowers." Dolen set the vase on the bedside table next to a bouquet of gladiolas that dwarfed his offering.

Happy squinted at the roses, fumbled with the bedside control and raised the head of the bed. "They're real pretty, Dolen, but they need water. My eyesight is still good enough to see that. Get some water from that there sink."

Dolen filled the vase in the basin by the bathroom door. *The old lady doesn't look like she's dying. What's Claudia's up to?* A few drops of water dripped on his shoe as he returned the vase to the table. "The receptionist said Claudia was here this morning."

"Yes, she was, that dear sweet girl. She has a brand-new book out you know. *Liar's Reward,* I think she calls it. She's on a book tour, but when I called, she came right away."

Dolen felt a flash of adrenaline. "You called her?"

"I sure did. I had the nurse bring me a telephone and help me with the number. Claudia answered right away. I told her my leg is still aching where I broke it, and I can't walk more than a half-dozen steps. I don't think I'll *ever* get to go home. It's time to dispose of all those antiques in my house before the rats get to them."

Claudia pulled into the circular drive of her grandmother's home and parked the rented Lincoln Continental by the walkway to the front door. She climbed out, stood a moment and gazed at the old house. It was a beautiful two-story craftsman style built in the twenties. But Happy and Morris Sidell hadn't purchased it until after Morris retired from IBM in 1960.

A sloping lawn covered half an acre surrounding the house, and beyond was a thirty acre orange orchard. Claudia had to admit that her cousin Clarence was an expert gardener and had taken care of the grounds like a professional. He'd been doing it since he was a teenager because Happy thought the work would give him a skill that he could turn into a business. But somehow it never worked out. Clarence worked part-time at Wal-Mart.

The air held the fragrance of orange blossoms, something that caused Claudia to recall a night years back when she sneaked out of the house to meet Julio, her first boyfriend, in the orchard. The memory brought a smile as she moved to the back of the car and opened the trunk. *He was a hunk back then. Too bad he turned out to be such a schmuck after I married him.*

She lifted out her suitcase and overnight bag, but left the two boxes filled with her novel for later. Though she hoped she wouldn't be in town for more than a week, she'd try to squeeze in a book signing before she left. Any bookstore owner would be delighted to have a big name author like her in his store.

Claudia approached the front door and as she climbed the steps, she glanced around the cement portico. A three-foot-square pillar graced each corner, and somewhere under one of the cross beams was a key. She put down her bags and ran her fingers along the underside of an oversized railing. After disturbing several spider webs, she finally located the key wedged into a narrow space where the beam entered the pillar nearest the door.

It took a bit of jiggling before the key turned in the lock. With the door open, Claudia stepped inside and paused to let her eyes adjust to the dim light. The house smelled of dust and old wood. Everything about the place was like stepping back in time, from the dark brown door casings to the glassed-in cabinets. And Happy Sidell's passion for antiques was evident in every room.

Claudia brought her bags inside to the foyer before she wandered through. The kitchen was her favorite spot. She'd spent many hours there assisting Happy with holiday meals. She half expected to see dirty dishes in the sink due to her grandmother's sudden hospitalization. But the kitchen was as clean as a TV commercial. She guessed that Clarence's mother, Wanda, had been in to clean. Or maybe Grand Mama had a cleaning lady. A pang of guilt niggled.

In truth, her grandmother had received little of her attention. Of course, she always sent Happy a copy of her latest book—plus flowers for her birthday, Mother's Day and Christmas. And then there was the occasional phone call. But those calls usually consisted of Claudia telling Happy about her latest success and

Happy chortling about how proud she was of her. Claudia had known little of what went on in her grandmother's everyday life.

Back in the foyer, Claudia clutched her big suitcase and dragged it up the stairs to her old room. There were four bedrooms on the second floor, one for each of the Sidell children and a larger one for her grandparents.

She opened the door. The room looked just as she'd left it almost twenty years earlier. After Claudia's father had been killed in Vietnam, Grand Mama had insisted that she and her mother move in and make it home. She'd spent a lot of time in that room, especially when her mother had been under treatment for breast cancer. Claudia opened the window that overlooked the orchard. A warm spring breeze drifted in, dispelling the stuffiness.

The amount of tragedy the family had suffered was nothing short of stunning. The previous generation of Sidells was all gone with the exception of Clarence's mother. And now, with Grand Mama past ninety, it wouldn't be long before the only ones left would be Dolen, Clarence and herself. It looked as though the Sidell name was going to die out. Clarence wouldn't be getting married. He was lucky to hold down his job at Wal-Mart. Dolen had a little girl. *What was her name?* She supposed that Dolen might marry again, though it was unlikely. He was such a slime ball; no women would take him if she had a lick of sense. For her own part, Claudia figured it was too late for children. Winston, her second husband, never wanted kids. His main interest in life was his publishing career and she agreed.

She opened her suitcase on the bed and hung her clothes in the closet. Afterward, she walked from room to room opening windows and soon the fragrance of orange blossoms filled the house. Claudia took a deep breath. *Okay. Where to begin? Probably with the small stuff, like silverware and dishes. I'll need my laptop and digital camera. I'll also need some help. I'm no expert on antiques. Tomorrow I'll have to find a dealer, get Grand Mama's stuff sold and get back to New York.*

Clarence Sidell was vexed. *Dolen always treats me like I got no sense. He shouldn't do that. We're supposed to be partners. He said when we got the money I could buy a new bike. I never shoulda listened to him. There's gonna be trouble, I just know it. I gotta figure things out for myself now.* Clarence parked his bike in the garage beside his mother's car and went in the back door of the house.

His mother, Wanda, was putting clean dishes from the dishwasher into the cupboard. The stress of her husband's death a few years earlier had caused Wanda to put on more than a few pounds, and nowadays the ties of her favorite Betty-Crocker-style apron barely reached around her middle.

The sound of the door caught her attention and she gave Clarence a smile. "Where've you been, dear? You missed lunch."

"To see Dolen."

Wanda paused with a stack of plates in her hand. Though she'd always liked Dolan's mother, she couldn't say the same about his father, and she didn't like Dolan's influence on her son. She placed the dishes on the shelf and turned around. "I'll fix your lunch."

"I'm not hungry, Mama."

The statement was so rare that Wanda wondered if he was ill. After wiping her hands on a dish towel, she waddled over to where he stood in the doorway and brushed his hair off his forehead. "What's the matter?"

"Nothing."

"Now I know better than that. You never turn down lunch. Don't you feel well?"

"Claudia's back."

Wanda's eyebrows arched. "Well, that's a surprise." Concern flickered across her face. "Is Grandma Sidell sick? Is that what has you worried?"

Clarence's scowl deepened. "Why would Claudia come back to Four Creeks after what she did?"

"Now Clarence, you mustn't be judgmental." Wanda opened the refrigerator and took out a jar of mayonnaise and some lunchmeat. "Claudia didn't know her husband was coming home early from his business trip. She thought he was a burglar when she shot him. She didn't mean for that to happen. It's a miracle he wasn't killed. 'Course, the fact she had another man in her bed didn't help matters any. Where did you see Claudia?"

Clarence's attention was divided between what his mother was saying and the sandwich she was making for him. He was particular about the amount of mayonnaise and mustard she put on the bread.

"Clarence? I asked you where you saw Claudia."

"I was gonna stop by to see Grand Mama when I saw her come out of the building and drive off in a new car."

"Did you speak to her?" Wanda placed the sandwich on a plate and handed it to her son before pouring him a glass of milk.

"No," Clarence said as he pulled out a chair at the kitchen table and sat.

"Why not?"

"I didn't want her to mistake me for a burglar." He took an oversized bite out of the sandwich.

No sooner had Dolen returned home from his visit with Happy Sidell when the phone in the kitchen rang. He lifted the receiver to say hello.

"We've got a problem," a gravelly voice said.

"I told you not to call me here."

"My contact wants the paperwork first."

"How much are we getting?"

"You'll get sixty grand."

"Only sixty? I woulda thought a '55 Buick Century like that convertible woulda brought more. At least eighty. How much was the deal?"

Silence.

"Oh, I get it," Dolen said. "You're keeping twenty for yourself."

"Look here, shithead, I'm taking the biggest risk. If anything goes wrong, this guy will never handle my merchandise again."

"Okay, okay."

"You got two days to come up with the pink slip. And get a signature on it too. Meet me at the same place at 11 o'clock." The line went dead.

Dolen hung up the receiver. *Crap! I shoulda thought of that before we boosted Grandpa's car out of the old garage. The pink must be someplace in the house. But where? And how am I gonna get in without Claudia finding out?*

Dolen slid his hand under his tee shirt and scratched his ribs. He'd have to talk Clarence into helping him with another crime. Even if he got his hands on the pink, his grandmother wouldn't sign it off. He'd need a copy of her signature to forge. *Maybe I could cut Claudia in. No. That wouldn't work. Ten grand would be chicken feed to her. She's got a penthouse in New York City.*

As Dolen stood with his hand on the telephone receiver, he remembered his grandfather's roll top desk that sat in a room at the back of the house. He dialed Clarence's home. When the call picked up, he heard Wanda's sweet motherly voice.

"Hi, Aunt Wanda. Is Clarence home?"

"Well, hello there, Dolen. How are you, dear?"

"Just fine. How about yourself?"

"Real good. We had a wonderful sermon in church this morning. It was all about honesty and The Golden Rule. Simply inspirational. You should come with us next week. I think it would do you a world of good."

"I'll think about it. Is Clarence there?"

"Is Grandma Sidell okay? I think Clarence is worried about her."

"I just came from a visit with her and she looked fine. Talked good too."

"Oh, that's nice to hear. Here's Clarence."

"Hullo," Clarence said.

"Clarence, meet me at the new ice cream shop in half an hour. We need to talk."

"Aw, I don't know."

"If you want that new bike, we got to figure somethin' out."

"Maybe I'll stick with the old one."

"Listen, you little fucker. You better be there, or I'll come looking for you, and you're not gonna like what I do to your face."

Thirty minutes later, Dolen sat at one of the little round tables in the ice cream shop with two chocolate ice cream sundaes melting in paper cups. He saw Clarence come through the door looking like Barney Fife on a bad day. His eyes were bugging and he was shaking worse than usual. His hand rattled the café chair as he sat.

Dolen pushed one of the sundaes in his direction. "Here. Gotcha some."

Clarence didn't move.

Dolen pursed his lips, about to do something he never did—apologize. "I guess I was a little hard on ya. I wouldn't hurt ya. You know that, don't ya?"

"You shouldn't call me names. It ain't right." Clarence lifted his chin and straightened his back.

Dolen reached across the table to pat Clarence on the shoulder, but Clarence pulled away like an abused puppy.

"Aw, come on. You're my buddy. We're partners."

"Partners don't call each other those kinda names."

"Agreed. I should watch my temper. Listen, I gotta plan and I need your help. There's something I gotta find in Grand Mama's house. I want you to be my lookout, just like before. I'm gonna go see Claudia and figure out the timing. Eat your ice cream while I tell you what we gotta do."

The next morning Dolen parked his car behind Claudia's rented Lincoln. He gave his cousin a momentary appraisal as she came out the front door of their grandmother's house with a laptop under her arm. Her hair looked like it had been styled with a leaf blower, but he supposed that might be the current fashion. The jeans and white tee shirt she wore hugged her body. He was surprised to see that she'd kept her trim figure. A quick calculation made her forty-two, an age when most women he knew were packing on the pounds.

He climbed out of his car and walked over to her. "You feel like doing something besides counting antiques?"

"How'd you know I was here?"

"I stopped to see our grandmother. She told me. She said you're gonna sell her antiques."

"That's what she wants. I've an appointment with a dealer. We're setting up an auction for Saturday. I was just leaving to show him some pictures of the items."

"How about dinner tonight? Give us a chance to get reacquainted."

Claudia scrunched up her face and shook her head. "Can't. I'm having dinner with the local writers group. Borders hooked me up with them. I have a book signing set for Sunday at the store."

Dolen lowered his eyes and gave a slight nod. "Sure. Another time."

"It's business, Dolen. The publishers don't promote books anymore. A writer has to do it all."

"Sure. I understand."

"I don't think you do. If I don't sell enough books for them, I'll be looking for a new publisher next time. It's a cutthroat business."

"No. I *do* understand. When's the book signing? Maybe I'll stop by."

"Ten o'clock. I didn't give them much notice, but they're doing their best to promote it."

Dolen nodded again and waved his hand toward the house. "I'd like to look around. Take a trip down memory lane, so to speak. Is the tree house still out back?"

"I guess it is. I didn't notice."

When Dolen started toward the house, Claudia put her computer in the car and followed him. As they walked through, Dolen remembered running up and down the stairway as a little kid. The twinge of nostalgia he felt vanished when he saw his grandfather's roll top desk through the doorway to his office. He walked in and ran his hand over the fine oak grain. "Will ya look at that? I guess you're gonna sell this too."

"If you want it, come to the auction and bid on it."

Dolen rolled back the top and made note of the papers stuffed in the cubbyholes. *That pink slip must be someplace in this mess.*

"Naw. It'd be too rich for my blood." He turned away and moved to the back door in the kitchen. Claudia trailed behind.

Out on the back porch, Dolen glanced at the garage and then gazed up at the old tree house. "Remember when we played Tarzan and Jane up there?"

"What I remember is that you had me hanging by a rope, let go, and I broke my wrist."

"You were supposed to land on your feet."

Claudia opened the back door. "I don't think I'm very good at trips down memory lane."

Dolen stepped inside. "Guess I better let you get back to disposing Grand Mama's precious antiques."

As the two trailed through the house, Dolen paused now and then, pretending to be interested in a special vase or picture. When they reached the driveway out front, he leaned toward Claudia, as if to kiss her cheek, but she pulled away and offered her hand instead.

"Nice of you to stop by," she said.

"Sure. I'll come on Saturday and watch the fun." He climbed into his car and backed out onto the street.

That evening Dolen coasted past his grandmother's house with Clarence in the passenger seat. The driveway was empty. Claudia had gone to dinner just as she'd said. He swung a u-turn, pulled into the yard and parked behind a tall hedge.

"Okay, Clarence. All you have to do is sit here while I'm inside and watch to see if Claudia comes back."

Clarence slouched in the seat like a spoiled child, arms crossed, his face pouty.

"If you see her car pull in," Dolen continued, "get out quick and tap on Grandpa's office window. I'll skedaddle out the back way. You understand?"

"You'll leave me holding the bag."

"No, no. It'll be dark soon, and we can drive out while she's in the house. Besides, she's selling books. We'll be gone before she gets back."

Dolen fingered his lock picks as he approached the back door. He figured it would be the easiest to open. He was right. He had it unlocked in seconds and left it open for a quick getaway. Once inside, he rushed to his grandfather's office and turned on the desk lamp. For several minutes he pulled papers out of the cubbies, glanced at each and replaced them. With no success, he turned to the drawers. The first one he opened held a metal box.

He pulled it out, set it on his lap and lifted the lid. The first thing he saw was the DMV address on an envelope. He almost giggled as he laid it next to the lamp. The second item was his grandmother's will. Putting the box aside, he flipped to the last page to locate her signature. Everything was going according to plan.

Earlier foresight had led him to stop at a local stationery store for tracing paper. Now he placed a sheet of it over Happy's signature and picked up a pen. As he leaned close to trace his grandmother's name, he grinned to himself. It was going to be so easy. It was a little trick he'd learned from his dad, who had spent time in prison for washing checks.

That done, he pushed the document aside and reached for a pencil to apply just the right amount of graphite to the backside of the tracing. Then he slid the pink slip out of the envelope, laid it on the desk and positioned the traced signature over it. He traced over what he'd written, leaving its shadow on the paper below.

When he'd finished, he tossed the tracing paper aside. He could see the signature clearly. All he had to do then was to follow the line and the forgery would be foolproof. Erasing the excess graphite was the last step.

As Dolen focused on tracing in his grandmother's name, a faint noise penetrated his concentration. He reached up, turned out the light and peered out the window to where his car sat. His instinct told him to grab the pink slip and make a run for it. Halfway out the door he bumped into someone. "Claudia!"

"Where you going, Dolen?" Claudia pressed her hand against his chest and gave him a shove.

As he regained his footing, a bright light from behind Claudia blinded him.

"You remember my first husband, Julio? He works for the police department now," Claudia said as she snatched the paper out of his hand.

A deep voice from the light said, "Turn around, Dolen, and don't even think about resisting."

Dolen knew the drill. An overhead light came on and handcuffs snapped on his wrists.

"Let's see what you've been up to tonight." Julio's firm hand guided Dolen back to his grandfather's office.

Claudia flipped on the next light and moved to the desk. "Will you look at that?" She picked up the tracing paper and held out the pink slip. "It appears we have before us all the evidence needed to put you in jail."

She was right. He was caught like a cockroach in a Roach Motel.

"You poor sap," Claudia continued. "If you'd simply read Grand Mama's will instead of forging her signature, you'd have known there was no need to *steal* Grandpa's vintage Buick. He always wanted you to have it, so she put it in her will for you."

Dolen groaned. "How did you know?"

Julio turned Dolen toward the door. "It doesn't matter. Let's go. We'll leave all this to the evidence team. I'll list the charges and Mirandize you at the station."

As Dolen was escorted to the waiting police car, a mockingbird in the tree house sang out, but no one noticed except Clarence, who stood smirking in the shadows.

SOUP DU JOUR
By Gloria Getman

Charlotte was confident that the noonday meal she was preparing for her father would please him. She'd baked fresh bread earlier that morning, and it was still faintly warm as she cut thick slices for his sandwich. The yeasty aroma made her smile. The way to a man's heart was through his stomach, her mother had always said. Charlotte certainly wanted to reach her father's heart as well as his stomach. She'd been planning her approach for weeks and time was running out.

She laid a slice of mellow cheese on top of the roast beef, certain the fragrance of the combination would make his mouth water. A white linen napkin served as a wrapper for the sandwich which she placed in the basket. She took a pitcher of milk from the icebox, held a Mason jar at eye level and filled it to the precise mark her father insisted upon.

Thomas Meier was a man of strong conviction, and there was nothing he didn't have an opinion about, even a simple meal.

She screwed the lid snug, and positioned it in the corner of the basket so that it wouldn't tip over, then added a firm, green apple. She paused. A cookie would be a perfect desert, but her father didn't believe in such treats, unless it was a holiday.

Charlotte topped the basket with a clean dishtowel before removing the white apron that covered her black dress. After she hung the apron on a kitchen nail, she picked up the basket and walked to the entryway of the house where she placed it on the oak table in front of the mirror, so that she could adjust her bonnet with both hands. As she tied the ribbons and smoothed her skirt, she examined her reflection. She nodded, pronouncing herself presentable for the public.

When Charlotte exited the snug Victorian house she'd lived in all her life, there was a lightness to her step. It was late September, but the midday was still warm enough that she didn't need a cloak. She longed for the time when she'd be allowed to wear something besides the dreary mourning dress with its long sleeves and high collar, but she wasn't going to let her attire spoil her day.

"Good Morning, Miss Meier." The deep voice came from behind a box elder bush in the garden next door. Horace Delk lived there. He was a newcomer to Pelterville, having owned the house on the corner only five years. He stepped into view with a pruning shears in his hand, his dark hair slightly damp against his broad forehead. His garden was always a joy to behold. He groomed it every Saturday, trimming off the spent blooms and pulling stray weeds. His rose bushes stood like sentinels on either side of the path that led to his door, the vivid colors standing out against the gray siding where Ivy grew nearly to the second story.

"Good Morning, Mr. Delk."

"Taking dinner to your father, I see."

"Yes."

"Here." He snipped a brilliant red rose, brushed his dirty hand against his jeans and handed it to her over the low wrought iron fence. His smile was genuine, and he was always polite, in the manner of older men.

Charlotte returned his smile. "Thank you." She raised the flower to her nose to catch the fragrance. "I'll put it in the basket. Perhaps it'll help put Papa in a receptive mood."

"I'd rather see it in your hair."

He paused and she felt his gaze. It almost made her blush.

"You take his noon meal to him every day. What is so special about today?"

"I'm going to ask him to write to Clover Woman's Academy. I want to attend next term."

"No fooling?"

"Papa couldn't spare me while Mother was ill, but now that she's passed on, I feel sure he'll give permission."

"Good for you. It's a big world out there, and you should see some of it before you settle down."

Charlotte suppressed a laugh. She wasn't sure that she'd see much of the big world, but with a teaching certificate she would be able to get out of Pelterville and away from her father's control.

Just then the noon whistle blew at the packing house. "I must hurry. Good day, Mr. Delk." As Charlotte stepped to the curb, the hem of her ankle length skirt swept against blades of grass growing through a crack in the sidewalk.

Shortly after Horace Delk had arrived in Pelterville, he had asked her father for permission to call on her. Thomas Meier had been irate and told Horace that his daughter was far too young, being only fifteen, for the attention of a man his age. Charlotte supposed Mr. Delk must be as old as twenty-five. She was glad her father had rejected him as a suitor. Her plans did not include someone like Horace Delk.

She hurried across the street and along Greenwood Avenue toward her father's bookstore. She dare not be late. Her father considered tardiness a cardinal sin.

Meier's Bookstore was over a mile from the house, and before long Charlotte was out of breath. She shifted the basket from one arm to the other and leaned against a post supporting the awning in front of Helm's Grocery Store. A sudden cool breeze swept up the nearby creek bed and made the canopy flap.

Charlotte gazed at the window display. Among the mixing bowls, egg beaters and jars of preserves, was a can of oysters. It brought to mind the day her mother died.

Louise Meier had been an invalid for the five years prior to her death, and Charlotte's dream of a teaching career had been set aside. Her father told her that it was her duty to care for her mother and maintain the house. She suspected he did not believe in education for young women, but she did not question his decision.

Charlotte didn't mind caring for her mother at first, but during the last two years, Louise Meier had become increasingly demanding and unreasonable. Charlotte sometimes wondered if her mother might be less irritable if her father spent more evenings at home. Often when she arrived at the book store with his dinner, he would inform her he would be working late and not to hold supper for him. Even though Louise Meier never left her room, his absence did not go unnoticed.

All of the housekeeping fell to Charlotte, including the garden and the care of the chickens. Charlotte reasoned that the family should have some hired help like most families in Pelterville, but neither of her parents thought it was necessary. Her mother's diet was particularly burdensome as she grew more finicky. Everyday brought some complaint about how Charlotte prepared the food.

The day her mother became so very ill Charlotte had polished the hardwood floors. Her father insisted the chore be done the first Monday of every month. It was hard work, a hands-and-knees job. She polished with a soft flannel cloth, putting fresh wax on the high traffic areas. By the time she was finished, her dark hair clung to her face and neck, and the underarms of her dress were damp.

As Charlotte climbed the stairs to her mother's room, she dreaded the fuss that had become almost routine. However, Charlotte entered the room with a smile. It was time for her mother's midday meal. "How about tomato soup and crackers today?"

Louise Meier was seated by the window where she could watch the street below. She wrinkled her nose and shook her head. "I have a yearning for oyster stew."

"But we don't have any oysters in the pantry."

"Go buy some."

"I have to fix Papa's dinner. There is not enough time. I am all sweaty. I would have to change my dress."

Louise's wheelchair whirled around. Her eyes narrowed. "Then get a move on. I said I want oyster stew."

Charlotte fled the room with her mother's shrill voice ringing in her ears. Hot tears blurred her vision. She scrambled to change and fairly ran the distance to the store and back. In the kitchen, heart still pounding, she warmed the milk, chopped the shallots and pried open the can. She had been up since dawn to build a fire in the cook stove, collect the eggs from the chickens, and begin her mother's care. She was tired and her knees hurt. It seemed like her life of servitude would never come to an end.

When the soup was ready, she carefully balanced the steaming bowl on a tray and gingerly climbed the stairs. She paused at the top, took a deep breath and tried to calm herself.

"Here it is. Nice and hot, just the way you like it." She placed the bowl on the tray her father had fashioned especially for the wheelchair arms.

"I am weary of this chair. I want to eat in bed today," her mother said.

Charlotte sighed and set the meal aside. If her mother was in her chair, she wanted to be in bed, and if she was in bed, she wanted to be in her chair. Charlotte lifted her so many times a day that her back never stopped aching.

"All right, Mother. I will help you into bed." Charlotte positioned the chair and blocked the wheels with wooden wedges. "Up we come." She grasped under her arms and lifted.

"Ouch. Don't squeeze so hard."

"Push up with your arms. You can help."

"My arms are weak. You know that."

Charlotte hoisted her mother into the bed, positioned the pillows and retrieved the tray, ready to place it on her mother's lap.

"I need the pan before I eat."

After another ten minutes of tugging at bed linens, fetching the dreaded pan and cleansing her mother, Charlotte presented the meal to her.

Her mother lifted the spoon to her lips for the first sip. "It is cold. Why do you always bring me cold soup? I am not French. Take it back and make it hot. And you forgot the crackers. I don't know where your head is, girl."

Charlotte returned to the kitchen and poured the contents of the bowl into a saucepan to reheat. She stirred in an extra pinch of pepper, a shake of salt and a special ingredient. She was careful not to let the milk scorch. After dishing it, she put a handful of saltine crackers next to the bowl.

When she set the tray down, her mother frowned. "I want oyster crackers, not these salty things." Mrs. Meier crushed the crackers in her fist and dropped the crumbs on the rug.

"You shouldn't be wasteful, Mama. Papa does not like it." Charlotte fetched the carpet sweeper from the hall closet to clean up the mess, then descended the stairs again and returned with a bowl of oyster crackers.

"Did you enjoy the oyster stew?" Charlotte asked as she offered the crackers.

Her mother gave a dismissive gesture. "Take them away. You are too late. I don't want them now." She wiped her lips with the linen napkin. "The stew had an odd flavor. Was the milk fresh? I have told you time and again, you have to be careful with milk."

"I am always careful. Perhaps it had a little too much salt." Charlotte cleared the tray and moved toward the door. "I'll have to hurry now if Papa's to have his dinner on time. You know how he hates to have his routine disturbed."

Louise Meier's funeral had been inexpensive, but tastefully done. Although none of her mother's family lived near enough to attend, a number of old friends paid their respects despite the sultry day.

September brought the relief of cooler nights and comfortable days, though the weather could be quite changeable. The Meier family drifted into a dull routine. Daylight hours grew shorter, and Charlotte had to work faster to accomplish her chores. She was not discouraged though. Today she would set her plans for the future in motion.

She slipped through the bookstore door in the nick of time, gasping to catch her breath.

Her father scowled at the pocket watch in his hand. "If you were better organized, Charlotte, you wouldn't end up here in such a state." He snapped the watch closed, returning it to his vest pocket. He took the basket from her hand with an impatient jerk.

Charlotte leaned against the counter, surveyed the numerous shelves of books and inhaled their unique odor. How she wished she could have books to read, not that she had much free time for reading. She had once asked her father for a book, but was informed that he owned a bookstore, not a lending library.

Her father glared at the wilting rose in the basket as he unwrapped the roast beef sandwich. "Where did that come from?"

"Mr. Delk's yard. I was hoping it would please you. I have something important to ask."

"Humph. I do not want you consorting with that man."

Charlotte felt her cheeks flush. She was not the sort to consort. After a pause she cleared her throat.

"Papa, I want your permission…." No, that's not how she wanted to say it. She took a deep breath. "Father, I want to go to school." She shook her head. That wasn't right either. She picked up the Mason jar, unscrewed the lid and handed it to him. She looked straight into his glaring eyes.

"Papa, please write a letter to the Clover Women's Academy requesting admission for me." The words tumbled from her lips. She explained her lifelong dream of becoming a teacher. She might have added that she wanted to be someone who was respected, but she kept that to herself.

Thomas Meier swept the basket she'd brought from the counter. The apple Charlotte had so carefully selected rolled under the counter.

"I will do no such thing. I will not have my daughter going off to some highfaluting school." His voice practically rattled the shelves.

Charlotte was astounded. She'd concentrated so hard on making her reasons clear, it had never occurred to her he'd refuse now that her mother no longer needed her.

"You might as well know," he said. "When the customary period of mourning has passed, I mean to wed the Widow Nelson.

She has two youngsters. You will be needed at home to care for the house and children."

Charlotte's knees nearly buckled. Her stomach churned. Arguing with her father was useless. Experience had taught her that. She reeled toward the door, fumbling with the knob.

Outside, the wind blew cold, twisting her skirt around her legs. Her mind was a tangle of images. This sort of thing happened to other people, like Bridget O'Malley. Her father had married a widow with four children, and his new wife was promptly in a family way. She died in childbirth, leaving Bridget to spend her life raising another woman's brats.

Charlotte noticed little as she trudged toward home. At Helm's Grocery, Mr. Helm was retracting the wind-whipped awning. He nodded to Charlotte. "Looks like we're in for a storm. A cold one too, I'll bet. Better hurry before you catch your death."

She barely acknowledged his warning, but hunched her shoulders against the elements. She turned her predicament over and over in her mind. There had to be something she could do to help herself; to confound her father's plan. Perhaps he could slip on ice in back of the house, and hit his head on the ax that always waited on the chopping block. What was she thinking? That would be murder. She paused, then turned abruptly and marched back to Helm's Grocery Store.

The bell over the door jingled, and Mrs. Helm greeted her with her usual warmth. "Hello, Charlotte dear. Aren't you cold without a wrap?" Without waiting for Charlotte to answer, she asked, "How may I help you?"

Charlotte smiled as she plucked a few coins from her pocket and pushed them across the counter. "I'll take a can of oysters and a box of crackers. I think this would be a good night to make oyster stew for Papa's supper."

TRASH DAY IN TULARE COUNTY
By Gloria Getman

Shortly before dawn on a Thursday morning, Iyla Zindorm woke from another bad dream, turned over and remembered that she'd neglected to put the trash cans out the evening before. For a moment she considered the amount of trash that needed to be picked up. The green and blue cans were about half full, one with lawn clippings, and the other with items destined for recycling. The regular trash held only one bag with chicken bones, coffee grounds and deposits from the cat box that would go to the landfill. Except for the weatherman's prediction that temperatures in the San Joaquin Valley would reach ninety degrees in the coming week, it could wait. But in a few days it would be stinky, so she decided she'd better get up.

She put on her pink robe and slippers and went out the back door. Her eyes felt scratchy as sandpaper, and she squinted against the morning light as she shuffled around the garage to where the trash was kept. Much to her chagrin, she found the gate that lead to the street was unlocked. As she pulled it open, she wondered how that had happened. It was unwise to leave your gate unlocked and your backyard available for any random thief to make off with your possessions. And besides, a month earlier the body of a murdered woman had been found in the city park. She gave a shudder and vowed to remind her husband, Malcolm, to be more careful.

Iyla pulled out the green can first and placed it at the curb. The blue one followed. She maneuvered it to allow the correct amount of space between the two, so that the long arm of the trash truck could manage them easily, and then returned for the regular trash.

When she gave the black can a tug, the weight of it was a surprise. She could barely budge it. What on earth had Malcolm put in there? She flung back the lid.

What she saw made her gasp and let out a screech. Her hand went automatically to her throat. Inside the container was the naked body of a young woman, folded in the middle, like a rag doll with her vacant eyes looking skyward. Her milk-white skin was shocking against the dark interior. Pieces of her clothing were tucked under her arm.

Iyla stared, momentarily frozen to the spot as though undecided what to do—a bad sign.

She recognized the woman. She'd seen her jog by the house nearly every morning just as the sun peeked over the Sierra. Though she didn't know her name, she remembered her white shorts and long legs, and how her honey-blond ponytail bounced in the morning air.

Iyla was an early riser, always up in time to greet Malcolm when he arrived home from work. Malcolm worked the night shift at a local cheese factory. He slept the day through, rising only to eat his dinner before leaving for work at nine o'clock in the evening.

It took less than ten minutes for police cars to arrive after she made the call. Before long her yard was swarming with uniformed men carrying measuring devices and plastic evidence bags. The street in front of the house filled with curious neighbors. The area beside the garage was blocked off with yellow tape and photographed from every angle. Iyla felt battered by questions the heavyset Hispanic officer asked. She wrung her hands as she felt his dark eyes note everything about her. She tried to answer his questions, but the whirlwind of activity left her dazed.

When he was finally satisfied, he turned his attention to questioning the neighbors. Iyla asked if she could go inside to make a pot of coffee. Permission was granted, and she fled to the security of her kitchen. As she sipped her coffee, she watched the commotion though the kitchen window, and was horrified to see an officer going through her recyclables.

Two hours later, the poor woman's body, encased in a black bag, was loaded onto a gurney and pushed out to a waiting hearse. The trash container disappeared into a police van.

No sooner had the neighbors wandered away when the phone rang. As she reached for the receiver, Iyla scowled when she noticed she'd lost one of her slippers somewhere that morning.

"I heard the police were at your house," a woman's voice said without a greeting. It was Morella, her older sister. "Was Malcolm home?"

What could Iyla say?

"No."

"I'll bet he wasn't at work either. You never should have married that man," her sister said for the thousandth time. "You deserve better."

Malcolm seldom stayed home on his nights off, but Iyla made excuses for him. He worked so hard. He was a good provider and he deserved time to himself. Though Iyla wondered where he went on those occasions, she never asked when he wandered in for breakfast. But this morning Malcolm didn't come home at all.

Iyla nearly wore out the sheets of her bed tossing and turning that night. It took an extra dose of the purple capsules her doctor had prescribed for her to sleep.

The following morning the doorbell rang at nine o'clock. When Iyla answered, she found two men standing there. Each withdrew a shiny badge from his pocket to show her.

The taller of the two introduced himself. "I'm Detective Frank Perez and this is my partner, Detective Milo Worley. We have a warrant to search your house."

Just like that, they were going to search her house, and there was no way to prevent it. It was like one of her bad dreams had come true. She stood aside and let the door swing open. The two men stepped inside. They were followed by two other men who nodded and went to work searching every room.

While the two nameless men searched though cabinets and drawers, she sat at the kitchen table with the detectives and answered the same questions asked previously. Did she know the woman? Had the woman ever been in her house? What was her husband's name? Where did he work? What hours did he work? And on and on.

"Where is your husband?" Detective Perez asked again.

The one question she couldn't answer was the one about Malcolm's whereabouts. "I don't know. He hasn't come home." There it was. She'd said it. It was out in the open.

One of the investigators stepped into the house from the garage. "Hey, Sam. There's a trap door to an attic out here." The other investigator followed the first man. The door between the utility room and the garage slammed.

"It's a storage area," Iyla explained. "We keep Christmas decorations up there. Plus camping gear and some old books too."

Several minutes later, the second investigator came in from the garage and went out the front door. He returned with a clear plastic bag. As he passed the kitchen door, he raised his eyebrows to the detectives sitting at the table.

Iyla's heart pounded, and she felt the blood drain from her face. She lowered her head. She could feel the two detectives watching her.

A minute later the investigator stepped into the kitchen. The bag in his hand was filled with clothes: a pair of white shorts and a sleeveless shirt, plus pink panties and a matching bra. Iyla's stomach churned and her head swam when she saw them. It could mean only one thing.

"Mrs. Zindorm. How do you explain Mary Burke's clothing in your attic?" Detective Perez asked.

Iyla raised her eyes. They were filled with tears. "I'm so sorry. You see, my husband is a vampire."

Earlier that morning, Detective Frank Perez slipped into a chair beside his partner in the report room of the Tulare County Sheriff's Department. He was a few minutes late. He'd stopped at Starbuck's for a cup of Latte. The room was buzzing with conversations between the men and women of the various sections. Most people were catching up on the news of the latest homicide.

A door at the side of the room opened, and Sheriff Whitfield walked in and leaned against the lectern. Two uniformed officers pushed a portable tack board into the room. On it was a map of the county with stickpins of various colors.

"Well, folks. You've probably heard. We have another one."

A groan emanated from the crowd.

"The body of a white female was found in a trash container beside a garage on Peach Street yesterday morning. According to the coroner, the time of death was sometime around midnight. We'll have definite information by Monday." The sheriff turned to the map. "Let's review what's happened in the last few months. On July 28th, the first victim, Melissa Long, was found at the fifty yard line of the high school football field. Thank God it wasn't a kid who found her. The street sweeper noticed her as he drove by making his rounds. He called the local police and their chief asked for our assistance.

"On August 23rd, the body of Grace Watson was discovered in the barbecue pit in the city park." He pointed to a square on the map. "And now this woman. It's a sure sign we have a serial killer on our hands. We've got to stop this guy before he has a chance to leave the area. It's our highest priority. Somebody knows something, so keep your ears open. Talk to your contacts. That's all."

Chairs scraped the floor, shoes scuffed against the tile, and the double doors in the back of the room opened. The assembly emptied out into the hallway.

"Perez. Worley," the sheriff called. "My office, please."

Minutes later Frank Perez and Milo Worley stood in front Whitfield's desk. "We won't have the detailed report from the coroner till Monday, but from what I've been told, this looks the same as the others. The crime scene techs are going over what they found at the site. Go talk to the Zindorm woman. You'll have photos by noon."

The two nodded and left. Out in the hall, Worley turned to his partner. "Did you notice each killing happened about a month from the other? It's like he can't stand to go longer than that."

Perez nodded. "By my calculations, the next one will be due at the end of October. We have no time to lose."

Iyla didn't sleep at all the night after the house had been searched. She lay awake waiting for Malcolm. It was almost daylight when she heard the front door open. She didn't bother with robe or slippers when she got out of bed to greet him. She surveyed his appearance. His clothes were dirty and his hair disheveled. His eyes were red-rimmed with fatigue.

"Where have you been?" she challenged for the first time.

"I told you before I left. I went hunting with George Winters." Malcolm shucked out of his coat and handed it to her. "We drove up to Lake County, thinking we might get a deer, but in the end we didn't even see one."

"You must be hungry. I'll make breakfast."

Malcolm gave a dismissive wave. "I'm not hungry, just bushed. I'm going to bed." He moved off toward the bedroom.

Iyla heard his boots drop on the floor and knew his dirty clothes would be in a heap nearby. She started a pot of coffee and waited. She didn't believe his story about hunting. She was sure he'd been hiding, waiting for the activity at the house to die down.

Before long, a snore emanated from the bedroom and she was ready. She took the sharpened stick out of the hall closet. It had once propped up a tomato plant. She'd washed it, but supposed a little dirt didn't matter anyway. She only hoped she was strong enough, and the stick was sharp enough to penetrate his chest.

She wasn't worried about Malcolm waking when she walked into the bedroom. He'd always slept soundly enough that her housework didn't bother him. She paused in the doorway. He looked so innocent lying there on his back, and for a split second, doubt flashed in her mind. But she brushed it aside. She had no choice. There was only one way to get rid of a vampire.

She moved to his side, raised the stick high and plunged it into his chest. Blood gushed out. Iyla stepped back against the wall. Malcolm gasped as the pain registered, raised his head for a second and then collapsed against the pillow.

It was over. She'd done it. She waited until he'd breathed his last, and then walked to the living room and called the police. She was certain she'd done the right thing because the police didn't believe her when she told them about Malcolm. She saw it in their eyes. They looked at her like she was insane. Now there'd be no more killings.

Iyla opened the door when she heard the sirens and settled herself in a cushioned chair to wait. Calmness spread through her body. A faint smile played on her lips. Though her nightgown was speckled with blood, she decided she'd wait to change.

Detective Perez was the first to bound through the open door. As he looked at her, she motioned toward the bedroom. The scene there needed no explanation.

The detective was back at her side in seconds. "You did that?"

Iyla nodded.

"Why?"

"I told you. Malcolm was a vampire. He killed those three women to fill his need for blood. I had to stop him."

"Mrs. Zindorm, your husband didn't murder those women. We arrested the killer last night."

"Oh, but you must be wrong. Malcolm did it. You found Miss Burke's clothes in our attic."

"No. You hid her clothing up there. On Thursday morning the first officer on the scene noted in his report that you were wearing only one slipper. We found the matching slipper in your attic next to the victim's clothes."

Confusion crossed Iyla's face.

"Stand up, please. Turn around and put your hands behind your back."

Handcuffs were snapped on Iyla Zindorm's wrists. As she was led out the door, Detective Perez could be heard saying, "You are under arrest for the murder of ..."

IN THE WAITING ROOM
By Suzanne Clevenger

It was by faith that Abraham obeyed when God called him to leave home and go to another land that God would give him as his inheritance. He went without knowing where he was going.

Hebrews 11:8

The words leaped off the pages of my Bible and penetrated my heart. I knew the Lord was calling me into a new area of ministry, but I had no idea what it would be. I'd been searching the Scriptures for inspiration and these words from Hebrews 11:8 caused me to stop and linger for a while and meditate upon them.

As I prayed, I heard a clear soft whisper ease into my thoughts: "You will be the Director of Women's Ministry." My immediate response was a sense of disbelief. I didn't have any idea how to begin such a serious calling. Indeed, there wasn't even such a position in our church. I thought of the many excuses regarding my lack of qualifications and experience. Yet the sense that God was calling me remained clear.

A few days later a package arrived in the mail. It was an audio series on how to develop a women's ministry. Where had it come from? I had no recollection of ordering it. I reviewed the contents of the package and began to listen to one of the audio tapes. It contained good, sound and practical advice. A work book was included. Was God confirming to me the words I had previously heard? I played Hebrews 11:8 over again in my mind. If this was indeed from God, then I knew I would wait and trust Him to fulfill this promise to me in His time.

And then the most amazing thing happened during the church service the following Sunday. An announcement was made that a search was about to begin for a Director of Women's Ministry. My jaw dropped open, tears filled my eyes, and my heart beat so loudly I thought the person sitting next to me could surely hear it. It took several days to fully absorb what had transpired: God's Word, the whisper in my mind, the audio series, and now an announcement I had not expected to hear.

I turned in my resume fully confident the job was mine. After all, hadn't I received a direct revelation from God? I was excited until the day came many months later when the announcement was made of the selection to fill the position—and it wasn't me. As unbelievable as it may sound, I wasn't disappointed—a little surprised maybe, but not disappointed. I felt at peace as I continued to hear the same affirming whisper when I prayed to the Lord later that day: "You will be the Director of Women's Ministry."

The woman who was hired had a lot of initials behind her name pointing to all of her qualifications and credentials. I lacked formal training in this area, and believed that was the reason my application had been rejected. I checked out several correspondence colleges, enrolled in one and was soon engulfed with books and homework. I wanted to be faithful to God and not let Him down, and I foolishly thought that God must need my help to fulfill His promise. If I needed a degree and initials behind my name, then so be it. I studied my books and wrote the required papers, but there was a certain uneasiness in the process.

Then, one quiet morning as I prepared to study, I heard the whisper again: "Put the books away. I will teach you what you need to know. You will be the Director of Women's Ministry." I really struggled with that one, but the whisper would not be silenced. A week later I collected all of my papers, binders, and books and placed them on the top shelf of the cupboard in my home office. I was immediately blanketed with peace.

Hebrews 11:8 filled my mind. It was true. I knew God had placed a special calling on my life and even though I didn't have any other details, I was willing to trust Him for the outcome as I prayerfully waited in His waiting room.

As days turned into months my hunger for God's Word increased. I studied the Bible with a new intensity and purpose, devoured books on leadership and understanding the needs of women. I listened to highly esteemed and faithful women God placed in my life.

A year after our Director of Women's Ministry stepped into her position, she resigned—naming me as her successor. I knew I was ready. I smiled as I prayed to God that day. He had indeed taught me what He wanted me to know up to that point. Even though I didn't have the qualifications of my predecessor, God qualified me in areas He felt were important: a willingness to have faith in Him as I waited, a love for the women I was to serve, and a dependence on Him to take care of the details. It was time to step from the waiting room and into the position God had called me to four years earlier.

God works in mysterious ways and His ways are not our ways. Have you ever felt He was calling you into a line of work, but the roadblocks before you seemed insurmountable? Relax. God is in control. Have you ever felt unqualified for a task you believed God was calling you to? God qualifies the unqualified. Have you ever felt left behind in an area of work or service. Be patient. If it's a calling from God, He may use someone else to escort you from the waiting room, just as He did for me. He simply asks you to obey Him and trust Him to show you the way in His perfect time. God never breaks a promise. He is always faithful to those who patiently wait in His waiting room.

All Scripture quotations are taken from the *Holy Bible, New International Version* (1999 edition) by Holman Bible Publishers.

OUR FUTURE IS SECURE
By Suzanne Clevenger

When the stock market plunged in late 2008, my husband and I, both retired, watched the security of our retirement funds all but disappear. Because of the apparent greed of certain people on Wall Street and a lack of attentive leadership in Washington, fear and uncertainty seized the hearts of millions of people both here and around the world.

My husband and I lost over half of our investments, a retirement package from which we hoped to live modestly, yet comfortably, for the rest of our lives. We realized that our plans for the future were drastically altered, and began looking for ways to trim the monthly expenses of our already conservative lifestyle. We were thankful that our home and car were paid for. Taxes and insurance remained our two highest expense burdens.

Thoughts of uncertainty filled my mind to the point that I was not able to get a good night's sleep. Then, as often happens in the early morning hours just before the break of day, the Spirit of God began to whisper into my mind, giving me words of reassurance. On this particular morning He reminded me of an event recorded in Luke 7.

Jesus, accompanied by His disciples and a crowd of people, traveled to a city called Nain in the southern region of the Galilee. How joyful this band of people must have been. They had seen Jesus perform many miracles—in fact a centurion's slave had recently been healed from a paralyzing disease, and Jesus attributed the healing to the centurion's faith. Undoubtedly there were skeptics and curiosity seekers in the crowd following Jesus, but there were also many who believed in Him because of His miracles and the authority with which He spoke. They had put their faith in Jesus—their hopes were high. Was this the Messiah the early prophets spoke of? Was the political arena about to change? Was their oppression about to end?

As they approached the city gates of Nain, a funeral procession was coming toward them. The only son of a widow had died, and the large crowd with her was on their way to bury him outside the city gate. The crowd following the widow was quite a contrast to the crowd following Jesus. One crowd was filled with hope and coming into the city; the other was filled with despair and leaving the city.

What would become of this widow? Where was her hope? There was a provision under the Mosaic Law whereby she could glean from the fields, orchards, and vineyards in the area. If she was resourceful, she might be able to eke out a living. It's also possible she came from another land. If that was the case, she might be able to go back to her kinsmen and seek help from them. But there is no mention of those scenarios in this biblical account. Her financial security was gone. In all probability she would become a homeless beggar living in the streets of Nain. Her future appeared bleak.

The incredible thing is that Jesus saw her. He didn't look at those carrying the coffin of her dead son. He didn't look at the crowd of people in the funeral procession. He looked at *her* and was filled with great compassion. Jesus looked beyond the obvious and saw the transparency of a mother's broken heart, suffering, and misfortune. He comforted her with three words: "Do not weep." Three simple words of assurance—three words signaling He was about to do something. I wonder what went through this bereaved woman's mind. Had she heard of this Jesus?

Did she recognize the hope in His gaze and in His words? Or were incredulous thoughts sweeping through her mind: "Don't weep? Don't you see that my only son has died? Don't you see that I have no one to take care of me? Don't you know I have no one to turn to?" But those words are not recorded. She was silent. Jesus moved into action.

He went to the coffin and touched it. Those carrying it stood still as Jesus spoke. The young man sat up and began to talk, his life was fully restored. The widow had her son back—hope replaced hopelessness. First fear and then cheers of incredulous joy rose from the crowd, and they began glorifying and worshipping God for the miracle they witnessed.

That's the way it is for all of us who encounter Jesus and allow Him to do the work He came to do in our lives. Luke 12:22-26 tells us our future is secure in Him. Jesus sees the uncertainties in all of the areas of my life. He understands the emotional toll this financial loss placed on my husband and me and so many others as we enter the twilight years of our lives.

But Jesus has the same amount of compassion for us as He did for the widow. He continues to reach out beyond the expanse of time and space and speaks to the transparency of our hearts, "Do not weep." Jesus touches us and life begins anew as God provides for our needs in unexpected ways. We are content.

I will lift up my eyes to the hills;
where does my help come from?
My help comes from the Lord,
the Maker of heaven and earth.
Psalm 121:1, 2

All Scripture quotations are taken from the *Holy Bible, New International Version* (1999 edition) by Holman Bible Publishers

NO ORDINARY DAY
By Suzanne Clevenger

"...you will call upon me and come and pray to me, and I will listen to you. You will seek me and find me when you seek me with all your heart."
Jeremiah 29:12, 13

She awoke to an ordinary day and set about her morning tasks, feeling a bit lonely and empty inside. About noon she picked up her water jar and began walking toward the well in the center of her village. Her neighbors talked in whispers to one another as she passed by. She instinctively knew she was the topic of discussion for the local town gossips. It had been that way for a long time.

As this unnamed woman approached the well, she saw a man seated nearby and recognized Him by His clothing as a Jew. As their eyes met, His looked so deeply inside her they seemed to penetrate her very soul. He asked her for a drink. She was a Samaritan woman; He was a Jewish man. Any self-respecting Jew would never speak to a Samaritan—a half breed with pagan blood running through her veins. She paused to wonder who He was.

As He drank from the cup of cool refreshing water she offered, He told her many things about herself and what He could offer her. His words filled her. They were intoxicating. They were liberating.

This woman of Samaria had just met the Messiah, the one the prophets of old had written about. His name was Jesus.

Leaving her water jar behind, she ran back to her village and told everyone she saw about this man and what He had said to her. She became an evangelist that very day, and many of the people from the village *"believed in Him because of the woman's testimony."* Others went personally to hear what Jesus had to say, and later told the woman, *"We no longer believe just because of what you said; now we have heard for ourselves, and we know that this man really is the Savior of the world."*
The Samaritan woman's ordinary day ended in a most extraordinary way.

Story based on John 4

* * *

Abby gathered up her few belongings and made her way out from under the bridge where she had spent another night alone and afraid. As she climbed out of the ditch, thoughts about her life weighed heavily on her mind. What had happened? How had she gotten to such a place of despair and what would become of her?

Alcohol and drugs had taken their toll on Abby. Falling to the ground, broken under the enormous weight of her addictions and pain, tears began to spill from her eyes until there were no more. All that remained was complete emptiness. She had hit rock bottom and the future looked bleak and hopeless.

As she sat on the ditch bank, Abbey remembered someone had once told her about a nearby rescue mission. Somehow she made her way there, and was met by the caring faces and actions of the staff and volunteer workers. They gave her a warm meal and clean clothes, and told her about Jesus and what He could do for her.

Abbey had been held in bondage by her addictions. Jesus, through the workers of the rescue mission, helped to set her free and gave her what she needed. Her ordinary day ended in a most extraordinary way because she made the choice to take the first step. Abbey was rewarded when others were ready and waiting to reach out to her, and gave her the hope she desperately sought—they introduced her to Jesus.

It has not been an easy journey, but now Abbey is well on her way to recovery as her faith in Jesus continues to grow.

* * *

The woman sat down next to me in the room full of people who came to hear Michael Reagan speak to the crowd at the annual Mayor's Prayer Breakfast. We chatted briefly. Her name was Janice. The room quieted down as Mr. Reagan stepped to the podium and began to give his personal testimony. He spoke of how he was once lonely, bitter and without purpose and direction for his life. Then someone told him about Jesus, and his life turned around as he chose to step out in faith, and accepted Jesus as his Lord and Savior. He made it clear that he is where he is in his faith today because someone once prayed for him.

I watched Janice out of the corner of my eye. She was fully absorbed in Mr. Reagan's message. A thought moved across my mind like a command: "Ask her. Ask her."

At the conclusion of the program two of Janice's friends came over to talk with her as she prepared to leave. I asked her if she had a church home. She shyly shook her head. "Do you know Jesus?" I asked.

Tears filled her eyes. "My grandmother's praying for me, and so is my friend here."

We talked a little longer and I told her I would be praying for her too. We parted company.

I don't know if I will ever see Janice again, but I do know without a doubt that Jesus is knocking on the door of her heart

(Rev. 3:20). I pray she answers Him and then one ordinary day will end in a most extraordinary way for Janice, just as it did for the Samaritan woman.

* * *

God's Word says: *"Build up, build up, prepare the road! I live in a high and holy place, but also with him who is contrite and lowly in spirit, to revive the spirit of the lowly and to revive the heart of the contrite"* Isa. 57:14, 15.

The Samaritan woman's ordinary day changed when she met Jesus face to face. Abby's ordinary day changed when she learned about Jesus through the volunteers at the rescue mission. Michael Reagan's ordinary day changed when someone told him about Jesus and he stepped out in faith and believed. And I believe Janice will one day experience an extraordinary day because people are praying for her.

Jesus is no longer here in bodily form, but He continues to change people's lives as we, His followers, make ourselves available to be used by Him. We are His ears to hear the voices of those crying in the wilderness, His lips to speak words of truth and love. We are His hands and arms reaching out to those in despair, and His legs and feet going outside our comfort zone to make *"disciples of all nations"* (Matthew. 28:19). Through us, He will continue *to "revive the spirit of the lowly and to revive the heart of the contrite"* Isaiah 57:15.

All Scripture quotations are taken from the *Holy Bible, New International Version* (1999 edition) by Holman Bible Publishers

MEDITATIONS
By Patty Sabatier

Vespers

Did you ever see a flower as its petals were unfolding,
revealing in this moment
its first and final purpose before it dies?
Does the flower know my recognition
of its fleeting expression of eternal beauty?
Does it care that I care?
Do our eyes meet in a moment of mutual recognition
as we pass?

There is a delicateness of life in these moments,
reminding me of the fine line between life and death.
How many moments in my day are like the flower,
revelations of my first and final purpose,
unfolding finite expressions of eternal beauty.
Tonight I pray to cherish the revelations of life
in the routine and ordinary that will never come my way again.

What I know of the evening
is the slowing down,
the letting go,
the long desired rest,
the coming home and the dying of the day.
Why can't I transition well from day to night,
from life to death,
like the flower that gently bows its head
to its wilting and dissolution?

Instead, at Vespers time,
I am restless
want sleep to come
without my conscious preparation and participation.

Patty Sabatier

This is the dark side of the life-death-life cycle,
hardest for me,
when darkness takes over the light of day,
when light bows its head to the yoke of the dark,
dominance by night's unknowing.

Is there a connection
between the daily failures of the arrogant and powerful ego
to notice this bowing of light to dark?
Does life take on the yoke of death for reason and purpose?

As I approach the surrender of day to night,
let my restlessness over unfinished tasks,
goals, and aspirations
give way to reverence
for the power and purpose of death and dying.
Let my arrogance that perceives life
only from my point of view,
holds so tightly to my way,
give way to the powerless position of reverence.
Enable me to take on rituals of preparation,
surrender that make the sacredness of evening real in my life.

May I learn to relinquish with peace,
integrity, and right order
my own conscious control over life and responsibility.
May I do this each evening
as a preparation for my final days and ultimate end.

May rest come easily to me each evening
with my willful yes to the brevity,
insignificance of my existence.

May every gesture I make in preparation for sleep
be an act of faith in the Dark Side of God,
the purpose of my unknowing.

Leaves from the Valley Oak

For allowing this mystery of darkness,
its reasoning,
to take hold of my evenings and nights
will surely lead me to the gentle embrace of death,
my final resting place,
refreshment.

The Rose
By Patty Sabatier

What is it about the rose that makes it so special?
What makes it stand out
from the Easter lily that ushers in new life after death,
or the daisy that reminds us of the importance
of the love-me and love-me-nots in life,
or the buttercup from my childhood that always revealed
with its yellow reflection on my neck that I loved butter?

Why is the rose above all flowers the choice
for expressing the inexpressible between lover and beloved?
Is it magic that captivates our senses
as the rose's maze of unfolding petals
leads us directly to its vibrant-colored, fragrant center?
Was it magic from its exposed core
that seduced the gods who created it
and have for centuries
placed the rose at the heart of mankind's fascination
with love and sensuality?

On Valentine's day, we choose the red rose
with its sweet sensual beauty
to proclaim our heart's secrets to the world
and a specific other.
A dozen roses seem to say how boundless,
how courageous our commitment is to give love to another.

Yes, mankind dreams of the ultimate expression
of its own fiery core
which can, like molten lava, flow out from our center
bonding with all that crosses our winding paths.
This total surrender of oneself to another is both joy and sacrifice,
like the rose that begs to be picked, sniffed, touched, adored
before it wilts and dies.

Leaves from the Valley Oak

Brief though its existence,
the rose, queen of all flowers,
powerfully, magically commands our reverence and attention.
May roses fill your senses
may you never pass a day without enjoying their beauty.

May you never be afraid of those prickly moments
when one faces the risks implied with surrender,
bold self-expression before the loves of your life.
In your bowing to the magic of the moment,
may you discover the grace and beauty
of the unfolding rose
as it silently releases its scent
into the life of your chosen ones.

The rose, with its magic, grace and beauty,
mysteriously captivates us all
as it connects one heart to another.
Choose to share roses
with another and experience together
this unconscious communion
between nature and mankind.

Just Before Dawn
By Patty Sabatier

Before the day-breeze rises,
before shadows flee,
at the darkest moment of the night,
just before dawn,
come, walk with me.
Walk in me.

In a gesture of stillness and a moment of solitude,
with precision and skill, embrace me.
Put to usefulness
the restlessness that haunts me,
drives me into wandering.

In my soul where there is no matter,
be what matters most to me.
Let my matter, my flesh,
my gestures of busyness
become real extensions of your fruitfulness,
the fruitfulness of our union.

It is beyond my knowing,
this moment you touch my soul,
like the forgetfulness of the infant
for life before birth,
the mother of her labor pains
with her offspring in her arms.

This fleeting reality of spirit and matter,
at one in the place I dwell from,
center of my being,
is known only in the aftermath of its touching.
Split second though it may be,
even, at times, only a gesture

Leaves from the Valley Oak

of longing and intent
like the fingers of God and man,
reaching, touching
this moment of touch,
this gesture of desire
the essence of all living,
remains the purpose of my life:
to live in the energy between us.

I will seek out the stillness of life
at the dawning of light,
knowing night,
the reflective background of the light,
is the requirement for light's emergence.

I will accept the unknowing
of this moment of transition,
the blindness I must endure
in my walk with you,
for which I long the most.

You are the breath within me,
the morning breeze when shadows flee,
I discover that I am loved,
cherished by the Light of Day,
energized by the shadows and the sun.

Sun, Wind and Rainbow
By Patty Sabatier

You are the Sun and Wind.
I am Rainbow.
I matter because I am a sign of the covenant
between Earth and Sky,
God and Man,
Spirit and Matter,
Sophia and Christ.
You are eternal,
I am moment,
like fire when the sun's rays are bent
through a prism onto the combustible.
I am a flash while you are forever Potential.

I will live but a moment.
Let me be transparent of the story,
the thread that is at the core of my life;
let me finish all that matters in my journey,
conception to eternal life.
Death and dying I know I must face
like labor and delivery.
The shedding of what no longer fits,
dry bones rattling with life because of your breath,
the phoenix rising out of ashes.

What is this fear I feel at times all about?
The ashes,
the shedding,
the rattling
all make me quiver in my boots.
Bloody bones and scary eyes are part of my living and dying.
Grant that I not spend much time
in the darkness of the birth canal
as I transition to eternal life.

Leaves from the Valley Oak

Let my shedding of what no longer fits be quick,
my fears and restlessness be short lived,
as I open my senses to the unknown.
Help me walk into the light
that must be done through darkness
for the sake of my essence in you
which is pure, and true,
without blemish.

Let me leave behind matter that energizes others.
Be it my painting,
my creative writing,
my efforts to bandage the wounds of others.
Let something of what I have given my energy to,
as I walked barefooted on this groaning earth,
be a source of life for humankind.
Let someone discover in the ashes of my living,
flecks of precious gold
to be saved and savored.

Joy in the performance of living
rather than the recognition of its successes
is what I hope to leave behind
in the dry bones and ashes of my existence.

There is a human hope for a pot of gold
at the end of the rainbow.
Rainbows show themselves in the most unique weather,
after storms,
through clouds,
on especially hot days
when rain is on its edge,
when sun and atmosphere unite in a most perfect manner.
May my life stand before others
as a sign that there is always reason to hope
in the midst of struggle,

that if not a pot of gold,
at least flecks of precious dreams and aspirations
can be discovered
by anyone who will search out its own end.

I am Rainbow,
I am matter,
I matter.
I am the result of Sun and Wind
bent through the prism of my existence
revealing hope and the intuitive fact:
life is worth the living and the dying.

The Authors

MARY MARTIN BENTON was born in Visalia, California. She has been involved in agriculture her entire life and continues to live on a walnut ranch near Visalia. She is the author of two novels, *Dulsey*, an historical, and *Winds of Time*, a Western. Benton is the recipient of the 2009 Lillian Dean Award at the Central Coast Writers' Conference for her novel, Winds of Time. Her short stories, *The Headgate*, and *The Grape Fields*, were both award winners in  the Central Valley Writers' Workshop Conferences in 2008 and 2010, respectively. Both stories have been selected for public broadcast on Valley Public Radio. In addition to the Visalia/Exeter Writers, she is also a member of the San Joaquin Sisters in Crime, Women Writing the West, and SLO NightWriters. You may visit with Mary on her website at: www.mmbenton.com, or email her at: mrybntn@aol.com.

Lianne Card has lived in Exeter for the past seven years. She has been a writer since childhood and now gravitates toward poetry and creative non-fiction. She feels that writing poetry about a place anchors her. Born in Winnipeg, Canada, she is a graduate of both the University of Manitoba and University of Toronto. At various times she has been a teacher, researcher, editor, and publisher. Her writing has appeared in anthologies published by Subud, an  international spiritual association and in local publications. Recently, she has begun to write tanka, 31-syllable poems in the ancient Japanese genre. She may be reached at liannec@netbox.com.

Suzanne Clevenger has been ministering to women since 1993 as a Bible teacher, women's counselor, and Director of Women's Ministry. She's also been a guest speaker at numerous women's events. In addition to having stories of inspiration printed in various women's publications, two of Suzanne's devotionals were published in *The One Year Life Verse Devotional* by Jay K. Payleitner and published by  Tyndale House in 2007. Claiming the biblical truths of Psalm 139 is what motivates Suzanne in her passionate pursuit to help women reach their full potential in Jesus Christ. Suzanne and her husband Ron live in central California and enjoy time with their four children and seven grandchildren. Quilting, knitting, and working in the garden are a few of her favorite pasttimes. You may contact Suzanne by e-mailing her at creekside7@sbcglobal.net.

Winnie Enloe Furrer majored in art and literature during college. Her photograph work has been seen in camping guides, publicity pamphlets as well as in magazines and newspaper articles. Her stories have been published in The Imperial Valley Press, San Diego Union, The Sentinel and the Fresno Bee. Her articles have appeared in several college journals and magazines such as Modern Maturity,  Visalia Lifestyle and Traditions. Some of her work is located in the Imperial Valley History Museum and a San Diego Mission Museum. In 1982 she retired from Pacific Telephone as a technical writer. Hanford became her home in 1999 when she moved from the San Diego area to be closer to her family. Winnie is a direct descendant of Delilah and Henry Akers, who settled near Kings River in 1853. She plans to write family memoirs about the Akers and other ancestors for her two granddaughters and five great-grandchildren. She may be reached at w_enloe@hotmail.com.

Gloria Getman grew up in Southern California and graduated from California State University Bakersfield with a BS in Nursing. After a twenty-five year career in nursing, she began writing in 1994. She's been published in Yesterday's Magazette and Reminisce Extra, won third place in the Central Valley Writers Workshop competition in 2007 with Soup du Jour and third place in the 2010 Lillian Dean First Page Competition for a novel at the  Central Coast Writer's Conference. She is a member of San Joaquin Sisters in Crime, SLO NightWriters and lives in Exeter, California. She may be reached at ggetman5592@verizon.net.

Donna Leach was born and raised in the central San Joaquin Valley of California. She is married and has three children. Donna has penned several short stories and enjoys writing mystery, suspense and horror fiction. She has been published in Lifestyle magazine and currently has a book, "Frightful Family Tales" available for purchase from Amazon Books. She may be reached at leachx4@sbcglobal.net.

Arthur Wallace Neeson was "writing" even before he learned to write."I made up songs and stories I later wrote down." He has written more than 200 pieces, including five hundred pages of poetry, a number of short stories and a short novel. He is currently working on a fantasy novel and an autobiography. A resident of the Valley for thirty-two years, he, his wife Joanne and son Michael live in Visalia. He may be reached at awneeson@mindinfo.com.

Sylvia Ross is an Oregon Trail descendant on both sides of her family, and she is one-eighth Chukchansi Indian. Much of her work reflects this California heritage. She is the author/illustrator of two children's books, BLUE JAY GIRL and LION SINGER. Her work was featured in *Sing Me Your Story, Dance Me Home*, an exhibit which toured the state for over three years. It has also been included in the anthologies: THE DIRT IS RED HERE; SPRING SALMON HURRY TO ME; THE ILLUMINATED LANDSCAPE, A Sierra Nevada Anthology; and in SEAWEED, SALMON and MANZANITA CIDER. She is completing her first novel. Sylvia is married to Bob Ross. They have four sons and five grandchildren. She early on worked for Walt Disney as a cell painter, returning to complete a degree from C.S.U. Fresno in 1969. She may be reached at thistles@ocsnet.net.

Patty Sabatier is a first time author and new to the Visalia Writers Group. She calls her style of poetry *Poetic Prose*. Patty was born and raised in Cajun country of Louisiana and spent some time as a Navy nurse and Catholic nun in Virginia. She has been a nurse for forty years and works now as a public health nurse in Tulare County. Her hobbies include painting with oils and pastels, her pets, gardening and creative writing. She may be reached at pattysabatier@aol.com.

John Noel comes from a long line of newspapermen, starting with his great-grandfather. It was this ink in his blood that brought him to writing at an early age. John worked for the Visalia Times-Delta and the Lindsay Gazette. He has also been published in educational and fitness magazines. His article *The Destruction of the U.S.S. Philadelphia* was the Grand Prize winner in the *Children's Writer* history contest. John was a teacher for 39 years. Working with young writers was his greatest love. John lives in Exeter with his wife Patsy. They have five children and six grandchildren. He may be reached at jrise@aol.com.

www.ingramcontent.com/pod-product-compliance
Lightning Source LLC
Chambersburg PA
CBHW070917180626
46817CB00003B/1098